<u>DNA –</u>

<u>DNA Trilogy Book 1</u>

by

Lynn Cook

Published by Juke Kick Publishing LTD℗
Grovehill Meadows Road, Crosshands, Llanelli,
Dyfed, SA14 6SF

www.gig-antics.media/publishing

Copyright © Lynn Cook Author 2015

Lynn cook Asserts her moral right to be identified as the
author of this book

www.lynncook.co.uk
www.facebook.com/lynncookauthor

Printed and bound in Great Britain by AMAZON

ISBN: 9781521415696

Separate Lives

Running Scared

DNA Trilogy Book 1

Family Business Trilogy Book 2

The Brother's Keeper Trilogy Book 3

Anonymity

Coming soon

Velvet Whip

About the Author

I was born at Ashford Hospital in Middlesex. I am the youngest of five brothers and sisters. i am a fun, outgoing person who is always up for a good laugh and a large glass of red wine. I am just like every other woman out there, I'm looking for my story, my Mr Right.

Initially I just wanted to write one book to be able say I've achieved this and able to cross it off my bucket list, which I Then I discovered I had more than one story to tell.

Now my ambition for writing is to inspire people to read the books I have published and have enjoyed creating. I would also like to reach out to future writers and inspire them to follow their dreams and tell their stories.

Acknowledgements

For Donald, Dennis and Eric

(My big brothers)

Thank you for never letting the wind blow on me and enabling me to grow up being as arrogant as I am. I love you for it with all my heart.

For my Mummy

Whoever said loss gets easier with time didn't have a mother like you, which I guess makes me lucky that I still, and always will, miss you with every beat of my heart.

Book Description

Monica Maxwell had spent years distancing herself from her past and that of her families. She had changed her name, her appearance, and unlike that of her family, earned her living strictly legitimately, much to her brother's disapproval.

An unexpected visit from a childhood friend intent on raking up the past was not what Monica wanted, but it soon became apparent to her that a debt was owed, and she had no choice but to comply. Getting her brother to agree with her, however, was going to be a completely different matter.

Chapter One

Monica Maxwell walked from the hotel reception in her full-length, black sequined evening gown, down the much used public pathway that led to the outdoor swimming pool.

As she predicted, at almost two in the morning it was deserted, although, at some point throughout the evening it must have seen some activity, as the one empty and the other half-full bottles of champagne and two glasses, one heavily covered in bright red lipstick, could testify. At five hundred pounds a pop, Monica couldn't care less about her guest's wastefulness, but made a mental note to remember to take it all inside with her when she left, as the littering could not be tolerated no matter how much money they had spent. Everything was always pristine at Hotel Eden and always would be.

She pulled down the zip at the back of her dress, stepped out of it and laid it on a nearby sunbed. She slowly walked down the steps in her underwear into the illuminated water, a little steam coming off the surface as she walked, she was reminded again of how much more she enjoyed the summer months here, enabling her to take her ritual nightly swim outside, instead of in one of the indoor pools.

As was her routine, she did her thirty lengths until she felt the tightness in her chest, and then rolled onto her back, allowing her breathing to steady as she looked up at the stars.

When her heartbeat had returned to normal, she rolled over into her dead-man's float position, allowing all of her muscles to relax as she gently floated face down on the top of the water.

Always, at this point, for the minute or two she could hold her breath, she would briefly reflect on her day until the last image she had of her mother would enter her mind. Perhaps it was strange that a five-year-old child, having found her mother floating dead in a pool, surrounded by the red mist of the water that had been her life's blood, would not go out of her way to avoid swimming pools for the rest of her life, but if anything, it was the one way she always found a connection to the mother she had once had.

Being as young as she was at the time, her memories were sketchy at best, and in most cases Monica wasn't even sure if they were real or simply things she had imagined, but this was the one thing she knew for sure. Her mother's last moments on this earth had been spent, face down in a pool; her life cut short at the hands of Monica's father.

One moment Monica's brain was verging on the macabre, the next all her senses were on high alert as something heavy broke through the surface of the water and before she had time to react, arms were around her waist in a vicelike grip squeezing out whatever little air she had left in her lungs. Her first instinct as always when she was touched without permission was to fight.

Bringing her elbow back as hard and as fast as she could, although through the water that she was now fully submerged under, it felt like she was moving in slow motion through syrup, she acknowledged contact made with what seemed like a face, and the arms immediately released her. Acting on automatic pilot, she pushed away from the unwanted intruder, or would-be attacker, she hadn't decided yet, but misjudged her closeness to the side of the pool, smashing the side of her head violently against the hard tile.

Momentarily stunned, and with the taste of blood in her mouth where she had split her lip, she felt the arms come around her again, although this time it seemed apparent that they were by way of assistance, as she felt her whole body being lifted from the water and unceremoniously dumped at the side of the pool.

Having recovered enough of her senses to know she was now in a position to breathe, she rolled over onto her front, raised herself to her hands and knees then proceeded to vomit the small amount of pool water she had consumed during her encounter.

Her chest heaved as she struggled to pull air back into her lungs, but she still heard the splashing of water as whoever her still unknown companion was, made their own exit from the pool.

"Ah for Christ's sake, I think you broke my goddam nose," came a voice muffled from behind her.

Having heard this in an American male accent, Monica decided she was not in any immediate mortal danger, but did not have the same feelings towards whoever this man was. Her golden rule of the customer always being right was about to be tested to its limits, as for once, she was not inclined to play nice. Her house, her rules, if she felt so inclined to break them.

As her breathing returned to some normality, although she was still panting fairly considerably, she felt a towelling robe thrown over her back.

"Do I look cold to you?" she gasped, glaring in what she assumed to be his general direction.

He huffed. "It was more a case of trying to spare you a little dignity. In case you are too drunk to realise it, you're practically naked."

She didn't recognise the voice, but could not miss the judgemental tone. She spat blood on the floor in front of her. "I'm bleeding; I nearly drown, and just threw up half the pool in front of you, do you really think I care right now that you are seeing me in my underwear?"

She slowly raised herself up on her knees and tentatively touched the side of her head that was now throbbing. Seeing blood on her fingers and fearing the worst she swayed slightly and felt a steadying hand at her elbow.

She shook it off annoyingly. "For your own sake, will you please just stop grabbing at me?"

"My pleasure," he barked.

Monica closed her eyes and took a steadying breath, fighting away the darkness and nausea that was threatening to take over her.   She turned to the stranger, feeling ready to have the confrontation he so richly deserved. "What the hell was all that about? You do realise you could have killed me?"

He had his back to her, and dressed in only a pair of swimming shorts, was wrapping a towel around his waist. "I thought you were drowning," he snapped in a manner that held no apology, and full of resentment at the inconvenience she was causing him.

"Then you thought wrong," she snapped back as she put a hand to a nearby sunbed and pushed herself up to her feet, closing her eyes again as another bout of dizziness threatened to overcome her.

He turned to face her with his hands on his hips. "Well, excuse me darlin', for trying to do the right thing, but it wasn't exactly my idea of a good time either if you know what I mean?"

Monica took a deep breath and mentally counted to ten, wanting nothing more than to tell this arsehole to go fuck himself, but not quite ready to cross that particular unprofessional bridge just yet, though she knew she was not a million miles away from that either. She opened her eyes and finally looked at him. All anger left her to be replaced by sheer astonishment as her brain registered the person standing in front of her.

"Oh, my God, it's you." She took an involuntary step back and almost fell over the sunbed behind her.

He threw his hands up in frustration. "Jesus H Christ, lady, how bombed are you? Will you please mind what you're doing, because I am telling you now, if you end up back in the pool, I for one, am not going in there again to get you."

She put a hand to her mouth and shook her head. "I can't believe it's you," she whispered.

He looked down his nose at her. "I'm sorry, have we met?" he said, sounding very unhappy about the prospect.

Monica gave a small half-smile, and then it all became too much, and the darkness that had been threatening her, finally overtook her.

Ryan Whittaker only just managed to grab the woman before she hit the ground. He stood there seething with her in his arms and let out an annoyed breath. He didn't need this right now. He had been nervous enough already about the meeting he was going to have tomorrow, so had thought a late night swim might help to clear his head and relax him, but he certainly hadn't counted on running into a practically naked woman, who judging by the champagne bottles he could see, was obviously drunk, and now, through no fault of his own, had suddenly become his problem. With the prices that this place charged, not to mention how difficult it was to get in here, he would have thought that they would be a little more particular as to their clientele. Perhaps she was a hooker; he thought to himself. She was certainly beautiful enough, and from the ample view he had got from her state of undress, had a body that would make most men he knew, reach for their wallets in double quick time, her discarded dress looked expensive, so yes, she was probably some high-end escort. He closed his eyes and cringed. If the tabloids got a hold of this story, his ass was grass. This situation was far too dangerous for him, but his conscience wouldn't let him just leave her there, so he would take her to reception and let the staff deal with her. If they called the cops and she got arrested, well, that was just too damn bad because it wasn't his problem, none of this was, and he was going to put an end to it right now.

As he carried her into the vast entrance of the sixteenth century stately home, now an incredibly luxurious, exclusive, five-star hotel, one of the night porters was the first to acknowledge his presence, followed immediately by the receptionist looking up from her desk, then instantly rising and running towards him.

"Oh, my God," she gasped, "what on earth's happened?"

It was an understandable question, but Ryan resented the hell out of the accusing stares he was getting from both members of staff. He dropped her on the nearest sofa, and then stood, pulling his shoulders back and calling on all the dignity he could muster, or that anyone could muster, given that he was standing before his judgmental audience in nothing but a towel.

"She hit her head in the pool, probably because she is so drunk she can hardly stand, that's what happened, and don't look at me for further details, because whatever company she had been entertaining, left way before I got there."

Wilhelmina Reynolds glanced in the arrogant American's direction whilst simultaneously crouching beside Monica, to try and get a better look at the damage. She may be the night manager, who took her job very seriously, but she was also one of Monica's best friends so could not stand by and say nothing while listening to malicious accusations.

"Actually, I think you're mistaken, *sir*, because she doesn't drink," she defended strenuously.

He raised his eyebrows. "Then I don't know what to tell you, because the way she was stumbling around, she must have had cause to celebrate and made an exception this evening."

"She doesn't make exceptions, sir; I'm not telling you that she doesn't get drunk, I'm saying she doesn't drink - ever," she replied firmly, but with her attention still on Monica.

Ryan was incensed by the fact that a lowly receptionist had just called him a liar. "So, you're familiar with her then? Why am I not surprised that she could afford to grease every palm she comes in contact with in exchange for a blind eye to enable her business to run a little more smoothly? Tell me, does she actually have a room here for the *entire* evening, or does she tend to book them by the hour? Just what kind of place are you people running here?"

Charlie, the night porter for want of a better word, as he was far more specialised in security than carrying luggage, but Monica never wanted uniforms to advertise that fact, took a step towards him, clearly unimpressed by what he had heard and more than happy to advertise that fact.

Wilhelmina quickly got to her feet and put a steadying hand on Charlie's arm. As much as she would love to see this particular guest get the shit kicked out of him, Monica's number one rule was never to be rude to the customers, only firm when absolutely necessary, and there were no exceptions to that. Anyone that worked for Monica for any length of time became fiercely loyal to her, and Wilhelmina could tell by the look on Charlie's face right now, that his idea of firm was going to involve some serious recovery time.

"I'll deal with this Charlie, you go and get the first aid box and call Dr Ezhill while you're at it."

Charlie was still glaring at the American. "Are you *sure* that's all I can do, Will?" His meaning was clear.

"Quite sure, for the time being, but," she gave his arm a squeeze, "don't go far, though, because I may change my mind."

He reluctantly walked away and she turned all her attention back to the American with a smile on her face that by no means reached her eyes.

"Now, to answer your first question, *sir*, she actually has one hundred and seventy-three rooms to be precise, she owns the place. To answer your second question, perhaps it would be best if you waited for her to regain consciousness, as *we* don't run the place, *she* does, and we only help."

She turned her attention back to Monica but not before receiving some well-earned satisfaction at the shocked look on the American's face.

Ryan composed himself quickly. "Are you telling me that *that's* Rebecca Katlyn lying there?" Composure or not, he couldn't hide the surprised tone in his voice.

There weren't too many people that knew that name in connection with Monica, but Wilhelmina was one of them, and although it surprised her to hear it come out of this stranger's mouth and sent her mind reeling a little as to how he knew it, she was not going to acknowledge this fact to him.

She looked back up at him from her renewed crouch. "Her name is Monica Maxwell, and you are?"

"His name is Ryan Whittaker, *Congressman*, Ryan Whittaker," Monica drawled, as she slowly opened her eyes and tried to sit up.

Wilhelmina put a restraining hand on her shoulder. "Stay where you are, Mon. You've banged your head and might have concussion. How do you feel?"

"I'm fine, Willie, honestly, just help me up."

"No," Wilhelmina shook her head, "absolutely not. Charlie has gone to call Dr Ezhill, and you are going to stay exactly where you are until he gets here."

Monica tried to pull herself up again. "I will do no such a thing. I simply bumped my head that is all, and then had a bit of a shock, but I don't need to lie down, and I certainly don't need a doctor."

"Mon, look at me."

Monica did as she was asked feeling she had no choice.

"Your pupils are somewhat dilated, your head is bleeding, you split your lip and you passed out. Now unless you want me to restrain you physically, which I swear I will if

I have to, you are going to stay right there until someone to whom you pay a huge retainer for moments like these, and who has a medical degree, tells me it's okay for you to move. Do you understand me?"

Monica let out a begrudgingly accepting breath. "Yes, Mummy," she whined sarcastically, knowing there was no point in arguing further with Wilhelmina Reynolds when she was in this mood, and besides, she may just have a point.

"Good," Willie acknowledged with a nod of her head, as she pulled the robe Monica had on back together, as it had parted when she had tried to sit up. "Now, tell me, was this an accident?" She spared a glance in the stranger's direction who had remained silent this whole time, although he was loitering close by, and congressman or not, Wilhelmina was still not impressed.

"It was..." Monica took in a deep breath as she looked at the face from her past for a moment and contemplated her words, "...a series of errors and misunderstandings, but nobody's fault."

Wilhelmina looked her straight in the eyes. "You're sure?"

Monica nodded and then winced as the movement made the banging in her head increase. "I'm positive."

Charlie returned, still looking very unhappy, with the first aid kit in one hand and an ice pack in the other, handed them both to Wilhelmina. "Doc's on his way. How you feeling, Mon?"

"Over pampered thanks, Charlie." She took the ice pack from Willi, gently laying it against her head, while pushing the first aid box away. "Would you do me a favour please, Charlie?"

"Absolutely, just say the word." He glared at the stranger, hoping against hope that the favour included kicking his arse.

Monica reached up and grabbed Charlie's little finger, giving it a shake to get his attention.

"I left my dress on one of the sunbeds out by the pool when I took my swim, and someone has left champagne bottles and glasses out there too. Be a love would you and go and grab it all for me?" She shot a glance at Ryan. "We wouldn't want someone seeing all that and think we're running some sort of bordello, would we?"

"Sure, no problem." He gave her hand a squeeze and walked away with a grunt, incredibly disappointed that the favour Monica was wanting was not more in the way of a physical nature.

"Willie, why don't you go and call the gatehouse to let them know Dr Ezhill is on his way, so they let him straight through."

She immediately looked back at the American. "Are you sure you'll be okay on your own?"

"I'll be fine I assure you, besides, Ryan and I need a moment alone."

She hesitantly got to her feet. "Okay, fine but I'll be just over there at the desk if you need me."

Once they were alone, she turned her head slightly, still holding the ice pack against it and looked at Ryan.

He was scrutinising every inch of her face, desperately seeking some recognition. "Rebecca?" he whispered to himself.

"I don't go by that name anymore, Ryan," she flatly advised him, "you need to call me Monica now. Is it a coincidence that you're here, or did you come looking for me?"

He stood there in stunned silence.

Monica clicked her fingers a couple of time. "Hello, earth to Ryan?" She waved her hand in his line of vision. "Anyone in there?" It made her anxious having him here and brought back far too many memories that she would sooner forget, so she wanted him gone as quickly as possible.

He slowly shook his head. "Sorry, I'm just a bit surprised. I thought that I would recognise you somehow, in some way, but I don't."

She huffed. "Why on earth would you think you would recognise me after all these years? The last time you and I saw each other I was five and you were twelve, and that was over thirty years ago."

He nodded. "You're right, stupid really." He drew his eyebrows together. "So, how did you recognise me?"

"I've followed your career, Congressman, I knew exactly what you looked like, now I don't mean to be rude, but how about we dispense with the pleasantries and you answer my question?"

He looked at the tendrils of hair around her face that were starting to dry. "I didn't expect you to be blonde." He was still lost in his own little world.

"I didn't expect you at all, so can we please just cut to the chase and you tell me why you're here?"

"Sorry." He gave his head another little shake, finally coming out of his daze and cleared his throat. "No, it's not a coincidence, and yes, I did come looking for you."

"Why?"

He raised his eyebrows. "Well, obviously I need to talk to you." His shock having dissipated, the arrogant tone was back.

"Excuse me for being a little surprised that after thirty years you feel like a bit of a chat. Whatever would *we* have to talk about?"

"Precisely what you imagine, I expect."

"Okay," she said sarcastically, "well, let's do that then. Hey, Ryan, do you remember the time when my dad killed your dad, and then killed my mum, yeah good times. So, nice talk, it's been great catching up with you, have a nice life."

He didn't look amused. "I'm going to need a little more than that."

Her patience was nearing its limit. "Then that's unfortunate for you because I seriously don't have too much more to give, nor am I inclined to with your superior attitude, which is quite frankly pissing me off right now."

"I didn't come here to pick a fight."

"I find that very comforting, if not a little insulting that you think you would be capable of taking me on, but then as we've already established, you don't know me anymore, do you? What is fortunate for you is that I happen to be the only one of my bloodline that isn't a bully or a homicidal maniac, because if you had approached my brother with this cavalier attitude, the outcome would have been very different."

He ran his fingers through his hair, let out a deep breath and crouched beside her. He raised one hand as if to place it on her arm but had second thoughts and rested it on the sofa cushion beside her.

"What I'm trying to say is that I appreciate what a shock my turning up here out of the blue must be, and for that, I'm sorry."

Monica's head hurt too much for her to be magnanimous, not to mention her heart, at his chosen subject matter. "You appreciate that do you because from your tone and demeanour I never would have guessed, but as long as you're sorry, then that just makes everything hunky dory."

"I've come a long way to have an important, civilised conversation with you. We are both tired, not to mention you're injured, so can we just meet up tomorrow and have exactly that?"

"What for, Ryan, why now? Why after all of this time, do you turn up at my home and want to rake up the past?"

"Please, Rebecca, it's important, I wouldn't be here if it weren't."

She glared at him. "I told you, I don't go by that name any longer. It's Monica now."

He contemplated her words. "So you've changed your name, your hair, any other changes?"

"I've changed whatever I could, Ryan, but unfortunately, DNA is a bit of a bitch and there is really no getting away from that fucker."

He raised an eyebrow. "You sound bitter?"

She smiled sarcastically. "Not at all, why ever would you think that? I love the fact that I was born to a murdering, drug-dealing, monster-gangster of a father, and a mother whose infidelity cost her not only her own life but your father's life as well. What I am bitter about, however, is a stranger, which is all you are to me now, turning up and making me think of all of those things, which, strangely enough, I usually put a considerable amount of effort into not thinking about."

"If my being here has upset you, I'm sorry, but it is necessary."

She glared at him again. "For the last time, Ryan, tell, me, why?"

"I will, of course, I will, but please, it's a long, complicated conversation, and this is not the time or the place. Will you please just meet with me tomorrow and I promise you I'll explain everything?"

Monica let out a deep breath. "Fine, tomorrow then."

He seemed relieved. "Thank you, I appreciate it."

"Don't thank me yet, I've only agreed to meet with you, I haven't decided to play nice."

He got to his feet. "What time would suit you?"

"Actually, never would suit me down to the ground, but I'm guessing that wouldn't work as well for you."

His face remained blank as he waited for her answer.

She let out a deep breath. "I'm always around somewhere so just ask at reception and they'll point you in my general direction."

He acknowledged this with a nod and then went to walk away but stopped himself. "If you do have a concussion you should wait until you've seen the doctor before you try to sleep."

She looked up at him with resentment in her eyes. "I don't think that stopping myself from having a good night's sleep is going to be too much of a problem right now, do you?"

Chapter Two

As expected, sleep eluded her for most of the night. The times that she did close her eyes, the pictures that invaded her mind, though whether they were actual memories or her overactive imagination she had never been sure, had her sitting bolt upright, grabbing her chest, and waiting for the panic attack to pass. Monica's whole life was built around control. It was the only way she could function properly and accept the hand that life had dealt her. All of the dreadful things that had happened in her life had been at a time when she was too young to control them, and to feel that control slip, even a little, sent tremors of fear through her, the likes of which she only ever experienced in her dreams.

With sunlight completely filling her bedroom she dragged herself out of bed, feeling even more lethargic than when she got in it. The lump on the side of her head felt like a bowling ball, the black eye and split lip that greeted her when she looked in the mirror, did nothing to improve her mood. Her private apartment was housed at the top of the staff wing, and consisted of three bedrooms all with en-suite bathrooms, a living room, a dining room, and a fully stocked kitchen, which was usually where she had breakfast alone each morning before starting her day, but today she decided she needed a distraction so wanted to go in search of some company.

Having used a very heavy hand with her make-up, for all the good it seemed to do, she made her way downstairs, chatted with a few of the kitchen staff while making herself a coffee but didn't loiter. Mornings were a very busy time for them as nothing was pre-prepared at Hotel Eden. Monica felt this was the least she could do with her cheapest room costing over a thousand pounds a night, so surely her guests deserved better than warm soggy bacon and congealed eggs.

She walked to her office through the timeless corridors drenched in the history of a time gone by. Portraits littered the walls of previous occupants, royals and nobles one and all, although some not so noble, with small plaques underneath each one with a synopsis of the individual's life and time spent within these walls. This house had seen its fair share of scandals since its erection, of this Monica was sure, apart from the five-star luxuries her guests could depend on, not to mention complete discretion which was a real crowd pleaser. If only they knew that the current owner was none other than Derek Katlyn's daughter, one of the most renowned gangsters of his time, or indeed that she was Nicholas Katlyn's baby sister, the property mogul, and international businessman whose interests featured heavily in the Fortune 500 list, not to mention notorious Playboy. He also embraced the memory of his late father and rejoiced in the fact that because of those well-publicised roots, he instilled fear in those around him. Monica had worked hard to distance herself from those connections and made sure that very few people were familiar with her background. She went by her middle name and used her mother's maiden name, wanting nothing to do with her father, his past actions, and demise, or anything he had stood for.

As she reached the reception area, she released an internal sigh of relief to see Willie had left for the day. Not only could she not take any more fussing right now, but she was also nowhere near ready to have the conversation that Willie would insist on, involving who the American stranger was and what was his connection to Monica.

She settled in behind her large antique desk and took her customary moment to enjoy the view out of her office window. In her opinion, the three hundred acres she owned were all beautiful, and she spent a small fortune ensuring they remained so, but this particular view was a favourite of hers. There was something about the lush greenery, the blooming flowers of all colours, the horses running loose in the pasture beyond, that never failed to relax her. Even in her current state of unrest, she felt her body take an inner sigh and managed to smile, regardless of her mood.

She forced her mind to turn to work matters and absorbed herself in it fully, attempting desperately not to think about whatever time Ryan was going to choose to make an appearance for the civilised conversation he felt they so needed. Try as she might her mind kept wandering. How she had worshiped him when she was a little girl. Being the same age as her brother, seven years her senior so a man in her young eyes, he had lived on the estate next to the one her parents had owned, which her brother still lived in to this day. She hadn't set foot back in that house since that fateful night so many years before, nor had she any intention ever to do so again.

Ryan and her brother Nicholas had been inseparable as children, and he had practically lived at her house. She would watch him for hours out of her bedroom window, or playroom window, or any window available to do some under-age stalking. She would try to tag along with them whenever possible, but Nicky rarely allowed it. Ryan, however, was always very sweet to her, telling her how pretty she looked in her new dress, or how lovely her hair looked in bunches, and she was absolutely certain that when she grew up and her daddy said it was okay, she and Ryan would get married and live happily ever after. All of that changed of course, along with everything else, after which his American born mother shipped them both back to the States, and she remarried, and where, to the best of her knowledge, he had remained ever since.

Two hours later there was a tap on her open office door and one of the daytime receptionists poked her head in.

"There's a Ryan Whittaker here to see you, Monica. He is telling us that although he doesn't have a specific appointment, you are expecting him? Is that right?"

Monica let out a deep breath and nodded. "Yes, Claudia, that's correct. Show him in for me, please."

She got to her feet and extended her hand across her desk ready to shake his. If a civilised conversation was what it was going to take for him to state his business and leave, then that was exactly what he was going to get. As he entered her office, Monica got her first real look at him, fully dressed now in a suit although he wore no tie, his dark blond hair brushed back from his face, cleanly shaven, and the same bright blue eyes she used to dream about so often. She would know those eyes anywhere, and no matter how much he had changed, how much he had grown, those eyes still belonged to the boy-next-door who she used to adore.

"Good morning, Ryan." She shook his hand. "Please, do take a seat. Can I get you anything, coffee, tea?"

Whatever opening statement Ryan had been expecting, it wasn't that. "Sure," he said hesitantly, "coffee would be good."

She held up two fingers to the waiting Claudia with a smile who nodded and left the room.

He looked at her face with its unsuccessfully covered black eye and swollen lip and he winced. "That looks painful. What did the doctor say last night after I left you?"

She gave him half a shrug. "It's more an annoyance than anything else. I've had far worse sparring with one of my personal trainers, I assure you, so don't give it a second thought."

He nodded at her not very subtle way of telling him she didn't want to discuss it any further and cleared his throat. "Let me start by repeating what I said last night. I do appreciate that my turning up here unannounced as I did must have been an incredible shock."

She smiled insincerely. "Yes, you did mention that before and as I already told you, that's a great comfort to me, Ryan, thank you very much."

He decided to ignore her sarcasm. "Truth be told, I was a little shocked myself at seeing you again after all these years, especially," he smiled, "at seeing quite so much of you."

So he was going to try to use humour to break the ice, fine, she thought to herself; she'd play. "Well, you were hardly suited and booted yourself there, Congressman." She looked him up and down. "Good job growing up by the way, very impressive."

His smile deepened. "And the same very much back at you. The black eye notwithstanding, you grew into an incredibly beautiful woman. Not that it surprises me, though, I always knew that you would."

"Thank you, Ryan, that's sweet of you to say."

Another tap at the door announced that their coffee tray had arrived, which was then deposited on her desk between them.

"Thank you, Claudia, and can you hold all of my calls and make sure we are not disturbed until I tell you otherwise?"

"Of course, Monica," she answered with a smile and left, closing the door behind her.

His face turned thoughtful. "I still can't get used to people calling you Monica. When did you change it?"

"As soon as I possibly could." Her face showed no emotion.

He acknowledged yet another shut down with another small nod. He looked around her office and then out of her window. "Well, it's quite some place you have here. You've obviously done very well for yourself."

His compliment sounded condescending and it annoyed her.

"Considering my background, you mean?"

He shook his head again and let out a deep breath. "No, I didn't actually. I know this is...awkward, but my sole purpose in being here is not to cause you any undue stress or complicate your life unnecessarily. Quite the opposite in fact."

Monica took in his whole demeanour and could tell he was almost as uncomfortable as she was but struggling to control it. She sat back in her chair and decided to throw him a bone, albeit a very small one.

"I believe you, Congressman. You shouldn't take my bitchiness personally. Considering people constantly surround me, I tend to live quite a reclusive life for the most part, and there's a very good reason for that, it's because I don't like very many people and I'm not a very nice person."

He seemed to consider her statement. "For someone who isn't a nice person, your staff seem to be very doting? They were very protective of you last night and rushed to your aid."

She half smiled as she leant forward and handed him his coffee. "You do get that I pay them, right?"

He accepted it with a smile. "I'm sure there's more to it than that. From where I'm sitting, you seem to have come a long way from the little girl-next-door who used to have tantrums at the drop of a hat, and do or say anything to get her own way."

She looked up as if considering his words. "Um...no, not really, I still do that from time to time when necessary. I just do it with hopefully a little more finesse these days."

"Then, in that case, I'll reserve judgement." He smiled as he took a mouthful of his coffee.

"As will I." She didn't return his smile. "So, now that the somewhat pleasantries are out of the way, well, as pleasant as I get anyway, why don't we get down to business, and you tell me exactly why you're here?"

He seemed to have trouble swallowing his second mouthful as he put the cup back in the saucer and the whole thing back on the tray. "Fair enough." He licked his dry lips, obviously choosing his words carefully. "As you already know, I am currently a United States congressman but I'm being lined up for the senate. It's supposed to be very hush, hush, so as with most things in American politics, it's practically common knowledge."

"Congratulations, Congressman, but what does that have to do with me and why you're here?"

He leant forward resting his elbows on his knees. "It's a means to an end, a stepping stone if you will, and the next step would be...well, the next step would be the White House."

Monica raised an eyebrow. "Impressive, but you didn't come all this way to brag, I take it, and not being an American citizen myself, you didn't come here to secure my vote, so why are you telling me all of this? What is it exactly that I can do for you?"

"Certain powerful people need to know I'm worth their while. They won't invest their time and money in me without putting every aspect of my life so far under a microscope. There can be no risk of a scandal coming out during my campaign, so any dirty laundry that there is has to be cleaned publicly first, and spun in my favour."

Monica knew where this was going now and could feel her blood starting to boil. "Ensuring you and your family come out squeaky clean, presumably." She leant back again in her chair. "Go on?"

"My...association with *your* family and the circumstances surrounding my father's death are about to become public knowledge again. I'm obviously talking about the American press, but given how prominent both you and your brother are now, there is no doubt whatsoever that the UK press will pick up on it too and run with it, I imagine."

Her face was like stone. "Are you kidding me?" she said very quietly.

He shook his head. "I'm sorry, no."

She rested her elbow on one arm of her chair then rested her chin on her hand. "It may have escaped your notice, Ryan, but I don't exactly seek out the limelight too much, in fact, I'm practically England's answer to Howard Hughes, so what makes you think I will allow you to expose me in this way?"

He raised his hands in surrender. "It's already done; I am merely the messenger. Wheels are in motion; you will be contacted soon and there's just no stopping them."

"So, you've already told these people that are interested in you, who, and where I am?"

"*They* told *me*. We are talking about the power behind the American government, Rebe..., sorry, Monica, and if they want to know something, they find out, and nothing stands in their way."

She looked out of the window for a few moments while the fingers of her other hand were tapping rapidly on her desk. "I've worked very hard to put my past behind me, Ryan, and because of your future plans, you came here to tell me that's all been for nothing?"

"I came here to forewarn you, and assist you in any way I can, in dealing with the situation if you'll allow me to?"

She turned back to face him. "You came here to tell me what it is you want me to say to them, you mean?"

He straightened in his chair. "I want you to tell them the truth, to the best of your knowledge. You were only a child when it happened, so any recollections you may have will understandably be vague, but I do appreciate that the fallout to your personal and business life will be substantial, especially given your efforts to distance yourself from...your past."

"My efforts, as you so glibly put it, amount to pretty much my whole damn life so please don't sit there and calmly tell me you appreciate the fallout, as you sound like an idiot because to be perfectly honest with you, Ryan, you haven't got the first fucking clue."

His face straightened. "That may be so, but I know how these people work, and to get through this quickly with as little pain as possible, you are going to need my assistance."

"Oh, so you're here to help me, well, that's nice. What I need, Ryan, is to be left alone. Can you assist me with that?"

He remained silent.

"I didn't think so," she sneered. "And as for pain, tread very carefully, Congressman, or I might be tempted to spread it around a little."

"Don't threaten me, Monica. It won't do you any good because I didn't get to where I am today by being easily intimidated. I suggest you take the olive branch I am extending."

"From what I hear, you got to where you are today by doing exactly as your mother told you. Even from a five-year-old's memory, I recall she was a manipulative bitch, so that obviously hasn't changed."

He looked indignant. "I'd appreciate it if you watched what you say when talking about my mother."

She raised her eyebrows. "I'm sure you would, but you see I'm also not easily intimidated, Congressman, and with the corner you have me backed into right now, I don't seem to have a hell of a lot left to lose, so I will warn you one final time about the attitude you adopt with me because, believe me when I tell you, you really don't want to piss me off any more than you already have or I will show you exactly what you can do with that olive branch."

"What makes you think you are in a position to warn me about anything? Your family closet may be full of skeletons, but mine is not, and I'll thank you for remembering that," he snapped.

"Well, let's discuss that for a moment, shall we, so we are both on the same page?" She leant back in her chair. "I read an interview your mother gave once, some time back now, probably when you were running for Congress, her being so involved in your campaign. She was asked about her time in England and about her interaction with my father. She stated categorically that she hardly knew the man and that their paths had only ever crossed once or twice. She must have forgotten the countless parties she attended at my house, not to mention the fact that, at all of those parties there were always several video cameras floating around that quite clearly depict just how well she knew my father, capturing the far more intimate moments than your constituents would like, I assure you, not to mention the thousands upon thousands of pictures there are, and a particular Kodak moment comes to mind, featuring your mother on all fours on the snooker table, snorting what I can only assume was cocaine off a mirror on the velvet, your father behind her, beaming a smile whilst pretending to fuck her up the arse. Priceless, wouldn't you say?"

He straightened in his chair. "Where are these films and pictures that you are speaking of if they genuinely exist?"

She gave him a tight smile. "They exist and are quite safe; I assure you. But while we're on the subject of your father, let us reminisce a little about the moron who, after meeting the most dangerous man he'd ever come in contact with, decided it would be a splendid idea to start fucking his wife. A pure genius, your daddy was."

"So your point is what, blackmail?"

"My point is, lose the fucking attitude, Congressman, or yours is going to be the shortest presidential candidacy in American history. You may think this is your chessboard, but don't suppose for a moment that I do not know how to play."

He was silent for a few moments then cleared his throat. "This thing is going to happen, Monica, and I couldn't stop it even if I wanted to. So, what are you going to do?"

She let out a deep breath. "I don't know yet. You're going to have to give me some time to mull things over."

"Not to push you, but the clock is ticking."

"I'm aware of that." She glared at him.

He hesitated over his next words. "I'm...I'm going to need to see your brother as well while I'm here. Can you arrange that for me, or should I contact him directly?"

She raised her eyebrows at him. "You want to meet with my brother? You can't be serious?"

"He's involved as much as you are, maybe even more so, given that he was a little older. It's only fair I pay him the same courtesy as I'm paying you and forewarn him."

She half smiled. "Have you any idea who Nicky is now? Don't for one second expect to meet the boyhood friend you once knew."

"I'm not naive, Monica, of course I realise he would have changed, but it doesn't alter the fact that I'll still need to meet with him and explain in a rational manner the series of events that are about to unfold."

She laughed out loud. "Oh, Ryan, you are more naive than you could possibly imagine. Don't believe for one moment that what you read in GQ or the New York Financial Times is all there is to know about Nicky. He's the same soulless monster my father was; he just wears a better suit. All the rationality in the world wouldn't stop him putting a bullet in your brain, if he even thinks you are going to inconvenience his life slightly in any way, not to mention talk badly about the memory of his late, lamented, precious father. We have very different points of view when it comes to daddy dearest."

Ryan shrugged. "That may be true but it's a conversation we need to have nonetheless."

She rolled her eyes. "And let me just count the number of ways that *that* conversation could go wrong."

"Monica, Nick is not the only one of us that's changed. Not only am I now a grown man, but I am also a United States congressman, and not without my own connections and resources."

"Nicky won't give a shit about your connections or your resources, and they won't do you much good either when you are pushing up daisies at Arlington, or wherever it is they bury monumentally stupid dead congressman."

"Then what do you propose I do?"

She let out another deep breath and buried her face in her hands, wincing at the painful reminder of the black eye she was currently sporting. "You're just going to have to leave it all with me, Ryan. Give me some time to get my head around all of this and do nothing until you have heard from me."

"How much time?" he pushed.

"Well, let me see." She raised her eyes to the ceiling as if thinking. "I need to formulate some sort of strategy to counteract the fact that you are annihilating my life, condemning my father, as well as stopping my brother from killing you, so I'd say...oh, I don't know, about twenty minutes?"

He slowly blinked at her sarcasm. "I appreciate..."

"Stop telling what you appreciate, Ryan," she interrupted him, "because you really don't. You are going to have to call your mother and tell her it will take as long as it takes."

He got to his feet. "My mother doesn't know I'm here, nobody does. I thought it would be better that way."

"It might be better for you if you didn't mention that fact to my brother if you see him."

"Am I going to see him?"

She looked shocked. "Is my twenty minutes up already? My, how time flies when you're having so much fun."

He remained silent, waiting for her to answer his question.

She took a mouthful of her coffee, enjoying the little control she had back by making him wait. "Nicky doesn't come here unless I invite him. We have an understanding in that we limit our interactions to times when it is absolutely necessary."

"So, the two of you aren't close anymore? That surprises me as he adored you as a child. No harm was ever allowed to come to his little Ecca." He smiled as he reminisced.

He was referring to the nickname her brother still used to this day from when she was learning to talk she couldn't pronounce her full name properly, so it always came out as Ecca and her brother had stuck with it ever since.

"Things change, Ryan. He still doesn't allow any harm to come to me, but only because of what it may do to his reputation, not through any real affection towards me. I'm going to need to call him, and I can't begin to tell you how much I *don't* want to do that, but given the fact that he will already know you are here, I don't see I have much of a choice."

He drew his eyebrows together. "How on earth would he already know that I'm here?"

"He pays people to spy on me. My staff are loyal, in so much as they do their jobs well, and with discretion enough to never speak to the press about the goings on here, but I can't screen for things like gambling debts, drug habits, or if they or a family member is in deep with a loan shark, so there are usually a few people around here that Nicky can exploit. I find them eventually and sack their arses, making Nicky pay them off with a couple of month's salary, and the game begins all over again."

He shook his head in disbelief. "How is paying people to spy on your family, a game?"

She raised an eyebrow at him. "You might want to hold back on the judging there, Congressman, given that fact of you standing here right now means you did your fair share of spying, and if you think that your mother doesn't have people keeping track of your every movement and reporting back to her, then you're not just naive, Ryan, you're delusional."

He held up his hands in front of him. "I meant no offence."

"Too late." She glared at him. "Now, just quit while you're only a million miles behind as I'm sure you have a few more million in you, and I will call you later when I have made a decision and have something to say."

He slowly nodded and left her office as she sat in silence contemplating her options, or lack thereof, and what her next move should be.

Chapter Three

For the rest of the morning, Monica pondered on the best way to handle her brother. Her own situation, while seemingly insurmountable to her, was very much secondary compared to how Nicky was going to react to this surprising turn of events. By midday, and still not having any sort of plan at all, she felt she could no longer put off the inevitable, so picked up the phone and dialled her brother's number.

"Well, well, well, I wondered how long it would be before I heard from my baby sister today. So, Montgomery showed up out of the blue, I hear. Is he making a nuisance of himself, perhaps trying to rekindle all those lovey-dovey feelings you had for him when you were a little girl? Has he suddenly realised that you are the woman of his dreams after all? Ah, come on, tell big brother all the embarrassing details," Nick chuckled.

Monica closed her eyes, took a deep breath and silently counted to ten. "I don't suppose you'd be interested in telling me who informed you of his arrival, just to save us both some time?"

Nick chuckled again. "You suppose right; that doesn't interest me in the slightest."

"You know that I'll find out who your latest mole is sooner or later, Nicky, I always do."

"Later it is then," he said with superiority. "Answer my question, what did Montgomery want?"

She refused to bite at his attitude. "It's Whittaker now, which I know you're aware of, but I don't want to talk about it over the phone. Can you drop by at some point, preferably this afternoon?"

"Wow, an invitation to the promised land, this must be more serious than I thought. If only I'd known it was going to be such a monumental day I would have worn my top hat and tails to work today."

Monica ignored the sarcasm. "Can you stop by or not, Nicky, I'm too busy to play games with you?"

"I'll see what I can do," he said flatly and disconnected the call without another word.

Well, that went about as well as she had expected. She gently rubbed her temples in an attempt to stay a headache that had been threatening all morning. She knew without doubt that her brother would come, he always did on the rare occasions she actually asked to see him, and especially now, if for no other reason than to find out directly from the horse's mouth what was going on, but he would never immediately accept one of her invitations, in case she mistakenly thought he was at her beck and call, and Nicholas Katlyn only danced to the beat of his own drum, always.

Although Monica was not prepared to tell Ryan the real reason behind her and her brother's estrangement, she knew deep down that Nick had never forgiven her for turning her back on her father after what happened, and he never would. To add insult to that particular injury, she changed her name and earned her living in a strictly legitimate way so she knew he felt she had deeply dishonoured the Katlyn's, which to him there was no greater sin. The final nail in her coffin she was certain, was the fact that when their father had eventually died in prison, his ill-gotten gains had amassed to millions upon millions, all of which, in accordance with his will, was divided equally between herself and Nicholas. This enabled her to lead the life she now held so sacred, so in one neat little sisterly package what Nick must see when he looked at her was, disloyal, self-righteous, and a hypocrite all rolled into one, and Monica couldn't and wouldn't defend herself against this opinion, because she agreed with him, it's exactly what she was. Having no idea when Nick would turn up and certainly no idea as to his mood when he did, she didn't ring Ryan to tell him she had made the call. With still no real plan in her head, the one thing she knew for sure was, that if there was any chance at all in making Nicky see reason over this whole business as painlessly as possible, then first contact had to be made by her alone, with Ryan nowhere in the vicinity.

Two hours later, having managed a slight reprieve to her mind's wanderings, she was taking her frustrations out on an unusually persistent client, or rather as he was hoping, a potential client, who just didn't want to take no for an answer. As a matter of course, any guest requests were handled by the booking office, where an immediate perfunctory credit check would take place, followed by an assurance that they weren't on the hotel's in-house shit list for any previous transgressions, but if the booking was large enough it was always handled by Monica personally. This particular client wanted to book the entire hotel for a whole weekend for a charity event, which ensured it was completely on her radar. At the initial request, having come from his head office's hospitality department, Monica did what she always did and checked him out and she was far from happy from what she had discovered.

Not only was Elijah Stone a self-made billionaire, this in Monica's experience would probably make him pompous, demanding, and full of his own importance almost to the point of intolerable for her, but he had also had quite a few run-ins with her brother on various business deals, each one outbidding the other and there was a real pissing contest going on between the two of them that Monica wanted no part of, not that he was likely to know that she was Nick Katlyn's sister. Those two points alone would have been enough for her to refuse his request, but to add to that, the previous charity events he had hosted were somewhat notorious, verging on hedonistic, and incredibly well publicised, all of which amounted to her not being remotely interested in taking his business. It was not a surprise to Monica that Mr Stone, apparently not used to being told no, persisted in the matter, but what did surprise her was that he was now writing to her personally on her private email address, though how he got hold of that she had no idea. That in itself would have been annoying enough, but to add to it, he was addressing her as though she were a child, listing all the good deeds his charities had done, because of course she would be too stupid to know the tax benefits that he enjoyed because of it, not to mention the publicity, and assuring her that any costs incurred to the hotel would be covered by himself personally. With the day she was having, she found it very therapeutic to tell him what he could do with his assurances and his money as her fingers bounced loudly on the keyboard.

"You look so fucking hot when you frown. It's almost enough to turn me straight."

Monica continued typing as a big smile covered her face. "As if anything would be enough to turn you straight, you big faggot. So, you don't call; you don't write," she moved the mouse and hit send and looked up at him, "where's the love, Vinnie?"

Vincent Marlon, all six foot two of him, pushed off the doorframe and came and stood in front of her desk. His barn door like physic would give anyone a run for their money, with his dark hair cut short around the sides and back, longer on top and hanging down in front of his bright blue eyes, and an angelic face always covered in a designer stubble, it made him appear like a gentle giant, which he was most certainly not.

This man-mountain made no secret of his homosexuality and because of that, he was intentionally meaner and more ruthless than anyone he came in contact with. On the face of it, he was Nicholas Katlyn's legal advisor and handled all his day to day business, whereas, in reality, he was an enforcer and his number two. He was also one of Monica's best friends. Despite Monica's reluctance to have anything to do with her brother's life, she saw Vincent as a kindred spirit, and despite his chosen career path, she saw a caring soul who had done what he'd had to in order to thrive in his dog eat dog world, and she loved him with all her heart, far more so than her own brother, and along with Wilhelmina, he was one of the closest people to her.

Vincent too saw Monica as the baby sister he never had and guarded her fiercely, and loved the courage within her. He thought her to be one of the bravest people he had ever met.

"Moani, Moani, you are the love of my life and you know it." He leant across the desk and kissed her straight on the lips as he always did. He drew back and looked at her and his face instantly dropped. "What the fuck happened to your face?"

Monica tenderly touched below one eye. "I had a fight with a swimming pool wall."

"And?" he prompted.

"And," she half shrugged, "I lost."

He took hold of her chin to examine the damage more closely. "Did you see a doctor?"

She brushed his hand away. "Yes, I saw a doctor; Willie wouldn't let me *not* see a doctor."

"So, what did he say?"

Monica took a deep breath. "In his deeply considered medical opinion, I have what is known as a black eye."

He leant forward again and gently kissed the bruise. "I worry about you here all alone. I wish you would let me keep a couple of guys around the place, just to be safe."

She rolled her eyes at the all too familiar topic of conversation. "And I've told you on many occasions that I have my own guys, Vinnie; one's who will only do what is necessary, and don't quite enjoy their work as much as yours do."

He half smiled. "There is nothing wrong with people taking pride in what they do, and doing it properly."

"There is with the prices I charge, to then have the crap kicked out of you because somebody doesn't like your attitude."

Vincent raised an eyebrow. "Some of your guests could do with a little attitude adjustment."

"I'd go so far as to say most of them could actually, but I'll settle for robbing them blind and leave it to their mothers to worry about their etiquette." Her laptop pinged and she looked down at the email that had just arrived and started to chuckle. "Speak of the devil; you just don't know when to quit, Mr Stone." She looked back up at Vincent. "I take it you know a guy called Elijah Stone, seeing as he's had some run-ins with Nicky?"

Vincent nodded. "I do, why, what's the problem? He's not here, is he, because Nick can't stand him? There's some real bad blood between them."

"No, he's not here, and nor is he going to be and that seems to be his problem. He heads up some charity for the underprivileged if you can believe that, and he wants to hold his annual fundraising ball here and I've repeatedly told him, no, but he just won't let it go. He's now suggesting that we discuss it over dinner. Can you believe the arrogance?"

Vincent's face became serious. "Would you like me to turn down the invitation personally in a way that will ensure he gets the message?"

Monica nodded. "That's precisely what I would like you to do, yes, and then if you could stick around and beat up anyone else who is mean to me or just generally gets on my nerves, I would really appreciate it, because I am, after all, only a helpless little girl who can't take care of herself."

"I'm well aware that you are more than capable of kicking anyone's arse who pissed you off enough, I'm just offering to help you is all."

"And I appreciate that darling, I really do, but I have this covered. What's he like, anyway?"

"Dragged himself up from the gutter, vicious when cornered, ambition off the scale, you know, the usual."

Monica raised her eyebrows. "So, a complete prick then in other words. Is he cute?"

Vincent half shrugged. "I'd do him."

She smiled. "You'd do anyone, you trollop."

He slowly nodded. "That's true."

"Talking of which, let's go away next month for a week or two. I've been looking at a hotel in St Lucia that I want to check out. I'm thinking about buying it and would like your opinion. We could get a tan, get laid, you know, the usual."

"You're on."

She got up and looped her arm through his. "So, back to the business at hand. I take it my brother is in the bar?"

He nodded. "He is."

"Did he tell you why you guys are here?"

He nodded again. "He did. The son of the guy your dad supposedly killed has turned up out of the blue and is making a nuisance of himself. Is that about the size and shape?"

"Essentially, yes," she confirmed.

Vincent shrugged. "So, tell me what room he's in and I'll have this sorted out in a few minutes."

She shook her head. "It's not going to be quite that simple I'm afraid, darling, and I'd appreciate you helping me to convince Nicky of that fact as well."

"Convince him to do what, kiss the guy's arse? You know Nick's not going to go for that, no matter what your dad did."

"This is serious, babe, and if we're not careful, it could get really ugly. The man we're talking about is maybe going to be the fucking president someday so we can't let Nicky get all up in his face. You really want the United States government looking into your business?"

Vincent seemed to take heed of her words, but to a man like him, backing down was never an option. "So let them look. Our arses are covered; I've made sure of it."

"Or," she took hold of his hand, "we could play this smart and get through it with as little pain as possible. The chances are the next few months are going to be uncomfortable enough as it is, and the papers are going to be full of all sorts of crap, so the last thing we both need is Nicky kicking off and making things a thousand times worse."

Vincent didn't look convinced.

Monica shrugged. "It's just good business, Vinnie. You know you can operate more smoothly without constantly looking over your shoulder, so don't put yourself in a situation where you'll have to."

His face relaxed slightly. "I'll help you convince Nick to listen to what the guy has to say, but as for the rest, I'm not promising anything."

She let out a deep breath. "Fine, well let's get this over with. You know my brother doesn't play too well with others when he's unsupervised."

Monica walked into one of the terrace bars she knew to be Nicky's favourite and found him sat at the bar oozing charm to one of the pretty barmaids who seemed to be intimidated and flattered all at the same time.

At first glance, you would be forgiven for thinking Nicholas Katlyn was Italian. His jet black hair, the image of their fathers, was always swept back, he had a natural build most athletes would be proud of, and seemed to hold an all year round tan, which he denied was artificial but Monica was unconvinced. Even the remains of scars above one eyebrow and the other cheek seemed only to enhance his good looks and having spent most of his younger life in some of the best private schools around, as Monica had, his speech did not portray the cold-blooded monster that he actually was.

One of the first things Monica noticed, apart from her brother in the thankfully, empty bar, was that his chosen muscle for the day was stretched back on one the sofas, a bowl of nuts on his lap, which he was shovelling in his constantly open mouth, while grinning at Nick at the same time who he obviously hero worshipped, with his feet up on an antique coffee table in front of him.

She walked over to him. "Yo, homey. You're not in your home now; you're in mine, so show some fucking respect." She kicked his legs off the table sending the bowl on his lap flying.

The natural reaction of this brain machine, whose IQ would not have reached double digits, was to jump to his feet in a pose ready to attack.

"Don't even think about it, big boy," she sneered, "I'll have you on your arse before you have time to raise your hands."

Nick chuckled from the bar. "Yeah, she would too."

Vincent didn't find it quite so amusing. He stormed over to the man and the slap he connected with his face sounded like it should have taken his head off. "What the fuck do you think you're doing? Go and wait in the car, you useless bastard, and pray I'm in a better mood when I come out."

The look on the man's face resembled that of a child that had been told off for misbehaving in class and he left without a word.

Nick continued to chuckle. "I see your unexpected guest has put you in a good mood little sister."

Monica scooped the remains of the nuts back into the bowl and placed it on the bar. "My good mood or lack thereof has nothing to do with Ryan's visit. I have asked you many times not to bring the brain dead morons you surround yourself with in here. Why do you do it when you know it pisses me off?"

He beamed a smile. "Because I know it pisses you off, and that amuses me of course."

She glared at him.

"Oh, what's the matter, Ecca?" Nick crooned. "Are you afraid that your fancy guests might be offended having to rub shoulders with someone who's actually done a hard day's work?"

Monica drew her brows together. "And what would you know about doing a hard day's work? When have you ever rolled your sleeves up and got your hands dirty?"

Nick smirked. "Plenty of ways to get your hands dirty, baby sister, you just don't want to hear about them as they may offend some of your self-imposed sensibilities."

She rolled her eyes. "Can we please just not do this today, Nicky? Let's get a table; I need to talk to you."

He half shrugged. "Let's talk here. I like the view."

He winked at the barmaid who now just looked intimidated after what she had just seen and heard and seemed to want to be as far away from all of them as possible.

Monica let out a deep breath. "I asked you here to talk, so if you're not going to do that, then you might as well just leave now, because I'm just not in the mood to play games with you today, Nicky."

"Very touchy," he teased. "Okay, fine." He jumped off his stool and kissed her on top of the head. "Bring me over another large gin and tonic would you gorgeous." He winked again at the barmaid. "Put it on my baby sister's tab; I think you'll find she's good for it."

She looked at Monica and waited for her nod before setting about her task.

Nick waited until they were seated and his drink was in front of him before he spoke again. "So, tell me then, what does Montgomery want and what has it got to do with me?"

"I told you, his name is Whittaker now, and it has been since he returned to America and his mother remarried, as you very well know."

Nick held his hands up. "Hey, stalking him was always your thing not mine, so I haven't got the first clue what he's been up to, but I do seem to remember something about his skank of a mother remarrying before her first husband was even cold in the ground. God, she was a cold-hearted bitch. Do you remember her, Ecca?"

Monica nodded. "A little."

Nick shook his head. "Nasty piece of work. To be fair, I never minded his dad; he was okay if she wasn't around. So, stop beating around the bush and tell me what he wants?"

Monica took a mouthful of the tonic water that was in front of her, knowing she would need as much lubrication as possible for the argument she was inevitably about to have. "The chances are he's about to become a senator."

Nick shrugged. "And?"

"There's also been talk that after that, he could make it all the way to the White House someday."

His screwed his face up. "Big fucking whoop. So did he come all this way for a pat on the back, or what?"

"No, he came all this way to warn us that the background check they are about to do on him will be extensive. His whole life is about to get put under a microscope, including his father's death."

Nick's face went blank. "Over my dead body. Better yet, over his."

Monica took a deep breath, expecting exactly this kind of reaction. "It's not that simple, Nicky. This thing is going to happen whether we want it to or not so you literally don't have much of a choice in the matter."

He looked at her with soulless eyes. "There are always choices, little sister; you just don't usually want to know what they are."

"Nick, will you please just listen to yourself for a second. You were offered a place at Cambridge, which you turned down, so I know you are not a complete idiot. This is not some back-bar bookie that you have caught skimming off the top. This is a powerful government official that could have Scotland Yard, MI5, and MI6 crawling right up your arse with one phone call. Do you truly want to bring that sort of attention on yourself?"

He smiled at her as though she were a child. "Ah, are you worried about your big brother? Better late than never I suppose. Trust me; I can handle anything he wants to throw at me."

"But why would you want to? Why put yourself in the firing line like that when you don't have to?"

"So, you're suggesting what? Just roll over and allow our family name to be dragged through the mud again? Oh, sorry, I suppose I should say my family name since you disowned it."

"That's got nothing to do with this."

"No, what you mean is that you think it has nothing to do with you, as you don't care what lies are told about us because you don't consider yourself a Katlyn anymore. And you seriously expect me to tolerate this, for what, some guy we knew a million years ago? Honestly, Ecca, I don't know why you would ever think I would agree to this." He drained his glass and held it up to the barmaid to bring him another.

Monica mentally counted to ten. "First of all, you love nothing more than to see your father's name in print."

"*Our* father," he corrected her.

She chose to ignore him. "Secondly, what lies would be told, Nick? You couldn't make up better shit than the actual truth of what happened, so why would anyone bother?"

Nick leant towards her. "Our father never once admitted to killing his old man, or our mother for that matter."

"He also couldn't deny it either because his whole defence was that he blacked out and couldn't remember anything. I may have been only a child, but even I remember how much he used to drink. Don't you think it was a little bit convenient for him to develop amnesia on that particular night, and let's not forget he was also covered in our mother's blood, and they were both shot with his gun that he used to keep hidden in his office."

"If you had once visited him in prison before he died, you would have seen for yourself how frustrated he was that he couldn't put all the pieces together and account for what really happened."

"Why would I have done that, to listen to more lies? What difference did it make whether I visited him or not? He had you, Nicky, his son, and heir; I was never of any particular interest to him."

Nick looked incredulous. "What fucking household are you talking about, because it's certainly not the same one that I grew up in? He adored you. You were the apple of his eye, his absolute princess."

"Yes, I've heard the stories of me being the gangster's princess, but it's not the way I remember it."

"Then you remember it wrong because it's the truth. Right up until the end you were all he wanted to talk about, never giving up hope that you would visit him at some point so he would get to see you again."

Monica sat up straight in her chair. "Enough Nicky. We've had this conversation before, many times over, but what's done is done, and I wouldn't change a thing even if I could, which I can't."

He slowly shook his head. "And everyone thinks I'm the ruthless one in the family. No wonder they call you 'she with the frozen heart'. Really, Ecca, how can you be so unfeeling?"

"It's in the DNA," she snapped.

They all remained silent while the barmaid approached and replaced Nick's drink.

Monica took in a deep, calming breath. "We are getting away from the point here, Nicky, and I need your assurances that you are on board for what's about to happen."

He smirked. "I haven't decided yet what is about to happen yet, but as soon as I do, I'll let you know."

She was fighting hard to keep hold of her temper. "You don't control everything big brother, no matter what you may think."

He raised one side of his mouth. "I control enough. The way I see it, if there's no congressman, there's no story - correct?"

"Are you completely insane? Haven't you heard a word I've said to you? You can't make a man in his position just disappear."

He nodded. "I've heard you. Our boy Ryan has become a real powerful man over the pond and with power comes powerful enemies. If the congressman's car was to...oh, I don't know, spontaneously blow up, for instance, why would anyone automatically point the finger at me? I may warrant a cursory glance, but surely no more than that?"

He went to take a mouthful of his drink but she stopped him by grabbing his wrist, spilling liquid all over his hand.

"I can't let you do that, Nicky. Can't you get your tiny mind around the fact that our family owe him, and this is our chance to pay him back for the great wrong that was done to him?"

He glared at her, the muscles in his jaw tensing as he struggled to control his temper. No one but his sister spoke to him this way. He physically relaxed, taking the glass with one hand then pulling his other wrist free, he shook the fluid on the carpet. "We owe him fuck all," he said flatly. "Why have you developed a conscience all of a sudden and being so set on playing nice with this arsehole? Are you fucking him or something, is that what all of this is about?"

Monica hesitated with her answer, considering for a moment whether she might have more joy going down this route. "Yes...yes, I am."

Nick's face broke into a huge smile. "Well, why didn't you just say that? So this isn't a favour for him that you want, it's a favour for you?"

She sat back in her chair. "If you like?"

His smile dropped into a grin. "You're lying. I can always tell when you're lying, and you're lying now."

She shrugged. "Believe what you like, but you've asked me a question and I've answered it."

He narrowed his gaze at her. "So how long has this relationship been going on?"

She cleared her throat. "I said we were fucking, Nicky, I didn't say anything about a relationship. As you quite rightly said earlier, I am 'she with the frozen heart' but does it truly matter?"

He kept his eyes on her as he drained what remained of this drink. "How is it that I haven't heard anything about this before now?"

She smiled sarcastically. "I can't answer that big brother, having no idea who your current spies are, but suffice to say I am not in the habit of discussing my personal life with the entire staff, so unless you have managed to coerce someone within my very limited inner circle, then it would be most unlikely for you to know the details of my sex life."

"They don't have to be in your inner circle to tell me you sleep alone in your apartment every night."

She raised a single eyebrow. "Again, sleep is not what we are talking about here. Wherever I choose to sleep, I do it alone, but what I do before I sleep, that's an entirely different matter, and we both know that appearances can be deceiving. I mean, let's just look at you for a second. On the outside, you look like a rational human being and a caring, devoted brother, when in reality we both know you are a complete psychopath who doesn't give a shit about me, except for appearance's sake and paying people to inform on me constantly."

For a split second, Nick looked genuinely hurt by her words and it surprised her a little.

He recovered quickly. "I actually think you mean that," he said quietly. "I do what I do because I worry about you, and as you tell me nothing, it's the only way I have to know that you are okay. I know we constantly have our little sparring matches, but surely you know when all is said and done that I love you, and there is nothing I wouldn't do to keep you safe?"

Monica rolled her eyes, not believing a word. "Bollocks, Nicky." She pointed to Vincent sat silently beside him this whole time. "He loves me; you just feel a certain sense of obligation and concern for your reputation if word got out that someone had the audacity to mess with Nicholas Katlyn's sister. That's not love, big brother."

He drew his eyebrows together. "Whatever have I done to make you think that?"

She faked a laugh. "I'm sat in front of you right now with a black eye and a split lip. In all of your worrying for my safety, did it even occur to you to ask what happened to me?"

"As you constantly point out, I'm an intelligent man. The fact that Vince is sat beside me right now as cool as a cucumber and not rushing off to rip someone's throat out, tells me there's nothing to be done. My guess is that you did it in one of your martial arts training sessions, or kickboxing, or whatever your latest fad is that makes you just a little bit dangerous. Am I right?"

"Not exactly, but I suppose it was self-inflicted," she begrudgingly acknowledged.

He raised his hands in an 'I told you so' gesture. "Then, far be it for me to interfere," he said sarcastically getting to his feet. "Anyway, this psychopath has places to be." He bent and kissed the top of her head again. "Good seeing you, Ecca, as always."

She grabbed his arm to stop him from walking away. "You haven't given me an answer, Nicky. For the first time, I'm asking you for a favour, now are you going to do as I ask, or not?"

He patted her hand condescendingly. "I haven't decided yet. Until I know whether you're telling me the truth and this is a favour for you, I can't give you an answer."

"And how exactly do you intend to find that out? Would you like me to give Ryan a call and drop down on the carpet right here and now and go at it with him in front of you?"

He squeezed her hand. "I'll find out don't worry, and I'll be in touch." With one final kiss on the top of her head, he walked out.

Monica turned to Vincent. "God, he's such an arsehole sometimes. What do you think he's going to do?"

Vincent shrugged. "I suppose that depends on if he finds out you're bullshitting him or not."

Lying to Nicky was one thing, but she was far too close to Vincent even to hope to get away with it. "You're not going to tell him, are you?"

He was silent for a few seconds then slowly shook his head. "No. I think you're right, and the best thing to do is to answer any questions coming our way, that's all public knowledge anyway, and get on with our lives."

Monica relaxed a little knowing that with Vinnie on board her chances of bringing Nicky around to her way of thinking just got a hell of a lot better. "Thank you, darling."

He got to his feet. "One thing I don't understand is why you are so keen to play ball. Nick's got his reasons for not wanting certain people to be digging too deeply into some aspects of his business, but you've got nothing to hide except who you are, which is all going to come out anyway. Where's the upside for you?"

She stood up in front of him and wrapped her arms around his waist resting her head on his chest. "Whatever Nicky chooses to convince himself of, Vinnie, we owe Ryan, or at least, our father did. His childhood was ruined because of my family so I really do think if we can help make his adult life run as smoothly as possible by simply telling the truth, then that's the least we can do."

"Even if it means sacrificing your anonymity which you've spent most of your life protecting?"

She nodded. "Even then. It's a big debt to repay so I'll do whatever it takes, whatever is in my power, to make it happen."

He rested his chin on the top of her head and held her tightly. "You're a better person than I am. I don't know why you say your heart is frozen; that's a load of bollocks."

"This has nothing to do with my heart; it's all about my pride. I don't want to be indebted to Ryan anymore."

"Whatever you say." He pulled back and cupped her face. "You're wrong about Nick, though. He really does love you and whether he tells you or not, he's very proud of you too, of all that you have achieved and of the woman you've become."

"He's too much like my father to love anyone, and as for being proud of me, he thinks I'm a hypercritical bitch with delusions of grandeur who thinks my shit don't stink."

"I'm not saying that he's a saint, but he adores the ground you walk on, Moani. My hope is that one of these days you guys can sort things out and perhaps spend more than five minutes in each other's company without the need to rip each other apart."

She smiled tightly. "I wouldn't hold your breath."

He nodded and kissed her on the mouth. "Take care of yourself, Moani, Moani. I'll make sure Nick doesn't keep you waiting too long, but it wouldn't hurt if you and this Ryan guy could be seen about the place a bit, doing things together, then maybe word will get back to your brother."

"Yeah I know, Vinnie, I'm on it."

Chapter Four

Ryan opened the door to his suite on her first knock. He had lost the jacket he was wearing earlier but still had the trousers and shirt on, the first few buttons opened at the neck, and Monica had to acknowledge again just how handsome he had grown up to be.

He greeted her with a smile. "Hi, come on in."

She took a tentative step forward. "Is this a bad time?" she enquired. "Maybe I should have called first before showing up at your door?"

Ryan chuckled as he closed the door behind her. "Is that supposed to be funny, considering how I turned up at your door?"

Monica pursed her lips. "Actually, it wasn't, but I do see your point."

"Take a seat. Can I get you anything?"

She shook her head. "No, I'm fine, thank you, and I can't stay long as I still have a million things to do before this evening, but I just wanted to stop by quickly to update you on how my meeting with Nicky went."

He seated himself on the sofa facing her. "So you've seen him already? Is he still here? Can I talk to him?"

She held her hands up. "Just hold on a second, Ryan. I told you before; this is not going to be as easy as sitting down and having a nice little chat with your childhood friend. You are going to have to be extremely patient and trust me to do my best to make this work for you."

He sat forward in his chair. "What does that mean, exactly? What is it that you have in mind?"

"It means my brother enjoys fucking with people's lives, especially those who want something from him. His first reaction was, as expected, not good. He pretended it was out of loyalty to my late father, which he has in abundance, unfortunately for us, but the bottom line is he just doesn't take too kindly to being told what to do, or that feeling of being backed into a corner by anyone. Much like us all, I suppose."

Ryan looked aggravated. "He does realise though that he doesn't have a choice in the matter? You did explain to him that questions are going to be asked, and regardless of his feelings for his late father, however misplaced, those questions will demand answers?"

For some reason that Monica could not explain and certainly did not expect, she suddenly felt some protective loyalty to her family. "I would be very careful about throwing words around like demand if I were you, Ryan, especially in front of Nicky if you do get to sit down with him. As you say, questions will inevitably be asked, but my brother's answers will depend solely on his mood and whatever small amount of goodwill I manage to inspire from him."

Ryan raised his eyebrows. "You mean when asked if he feels so inclined, he'll lie?"

"No, I mean for once in his life, when asked if he feels so inclined, he might tell the truth, the whole truth, and nothing but the truth. While the Montgomery's were never in the Katlyn's league for bad deeds, let's not forget that your parents' behaviour when socialising with mine, was not exactly conducive to polite society either and I would imagine that would go down very badly with the voters. Believe me; Nicky has an abundance of proof of such behaviour."

Ryan looked indignant. "You've already made this point quite succinctly earlier today."

"Well, I'm making it again, and don't insult me by pretending you don't know what I'm talking about, or pretending that this is all news to you, because whatever stories I know, you know, so don't go off half-cocked thinking you hold all the cards, because you don't. It may be too late to do your father any real harm, but I would bet everything I own that your mother would not appreciate her current circle of friends becoming too familiar with her past. If your parents were half the people they pretended to be they wouldn't have been within a million miles of my family, so don't forget there are some truths you just don't want coming out, and for the sake of your career, I would treat Nicky with kid gloves if I were you. Trust me; neither you nor your mother will like the outcome if you don't."

Ryan took a deep breath as he contemplated her words. "So, what do you suggest I do?"

"I've already told you what you need to do. You need to leave me to try and convince my brother to play nice. He wasn't exactly amenable to doing you any favours, but there is a very slight chance that he might do me one, if for no other reason than to have me in his debt, but as I have already explained, Nicky and I aren't exactly close anymore."

He nodded slowly. "Strangely enough, I think that's been the biggest shock of all to me. God, how he loved you when we were children."

"He doesn't anymore, I assure you. We hugely disapprove of each other's lives; we have nothing in common, and we make no secret of it. Having said that, and fortunately for the two of us right now, he does like to give the impression that he cares for me, even to those closest to him, and that might be enough for him to keep his mouth shut."

He sat back in his seat and crossed his legs. "So, what's the plan? How do we move forward?"

"I've told him that we are together right now and that that's why I want him to help you with the next step of your career."

Ryan's eyes immediately widened. "You've done what?"

Monica leant back against the sofa, refusing to feel embarrassed or ashamed of her little ruse. "I think you heard me, Ryan. I wasn't getting anywhere trying to appeal to his better nature, mainly because he doesn't have one, so instead I told him that you are my current sexual partner and that this wasn't about helping you, it was about helping me."

He looked a little confused. "Your current sexual partner? That seems an odd way to call someone your lover. So let me get this straight." He grinned. "You weren't getting your own way, so you had one of those adult tantrums you told me about?"

She raised one side of her mouth. "Something like that, yes."

"Okay." He ran his fingers through his hair. "So basically, if he asks me, I have to pretend that you and I are at it like bunnies, and then hopefully it will be plain sailing?"

She leant her head back, closing her eyes and pinching the bridge of her nose, still trying to hold off the persistent threat of a migraine. "As with most things involving my brother, it's not going to be that simple, mainly because he doesn't believe me yet."

"Meaning what?"

She raised her head and looked at him. "Meaning, I'm afraid you and I are going to have to put on a bit of a show."

Ryan looked concerned. "I'm not sure I know exactly what that means. What do you mean by putting on a bit of a show, precisely? Holding hands in front of him, whispering sweet nothings into each other's ears, what?"

Monica breathed out a laugh. "Hardly. If I were to be all gushy towards you or let you be all gushy towards me for that matter, my brother would know in a second that it was all total crap. Besides, the show's not for him; it's for whichever members of my staff he is currently paying for information. Unfortunately, I have no idea who that might be right now, or how many there are because knowing Nicky, he wouldn't put all his eggs in one basket."

"I still have no idea what we're talking about here."

"Essentially, we would have to act like we were together in front of the entire staff, but in a subtle enough way for it to be believed. I'm not a very tactile person, Ryan, which is very well known, and I certainly do not do any public displays of affection, so it would be all about the sly looks when we pretend we don't know anyone is watching, the chaste kisses when we get caught accidently, that sort of thing, and of course be seen together as much as possible. It's tedious, I know, but there's just no other way around it."

Ryan looked astounded. "Have you any idea how crazy what you're suggesting is? We're not children anymore, Monica, that can just play dress up whenever the mood takes us. This isn't a game we're playing here, it's my life, and I can't speak for you, but my actions have consequences, so I'm not about to jump out of the frying pan, into the fire."

Monica's temper that she had been holding onto by a thread, finally escaped her. "You sanctimonious bastard. Have you any idea how much I am putting myself out for you right now? Do you have the slightest clue how much I've been prepared to sacrifice to make your life easier? Can you even slightly comprehend how far-reaching and life-altering the consequences to me will be if we manage to pull this off?" She got to her feet. "You know what, Ryan, fuck it. You deal with Nicky, yourself, as you think you'll do a better job of it. I'm fairly sure that it will result in either Nicky owning your arse or you being unemployed, but maybe I'll be wrong. You be sure to let me know how it works out for you and have a safe journey home." She walked towards the door.

"Monica, wait." He jumped to his feet.

She stood with her hand on the door handle. "What?" she said through gritted teeth.

"I'm sorry, I was out of line. Please, come and sit back down and let's finish our conversation."

She turned and faced him leaning against the door. "I'll stand because unless there is an immediate attitude adjustment from you, this conversation is almost over."

"Please. Let me fix us both a drink." He walked over to the bar. "What can I get for you?"

"Some humility would be nice. Make it a double." She smiled tartly.

He took this reprimand in silence while pouring himself a whisky, downing it in one before turning to face her again. "I know how ungrateful I must sound, it's just my life, everything I do, it's under such scrutiny, so I always have to be so careful of my actions. And there's...well, there's someone in my life that..."

"You mean the governor's daughter, I presume?" Monica clarified.

He seemed a little shocked and unsure how to answer. "Meredith and I...we..."

"You don't have to explain anything to me, Ryan. She no doubt comes from the right family with the right background. She knows your world and the people in it and has never done anything in her whole life to raise an eyebrow. An excellent choice for first lady. I don't know, of course, how open and honest your relationship is with this woman, but tell her what's going on, or don't, it's entirely up to you. My staff, while seemingly susceptible to my brother's powers of persuasion, would never risk talking to the press. They earn a good living here, not to mention the prestige that comes with working at one of the most exclusive hotels in England. They wouldn't jeopardise their positions or risk my brother's wrath for that matter for what he would consider an affront to his sister. Journalists can be bought into revealing their sources; my brother cannot. With the exception of Nicky, everything that goes on within the walls of Hotel Eden, very much stays here. My guests would expect nor accept anything less."

He poured himself another drink, again swallowing it in one before turning to face her. "Why are you doing this?"

"I told you, I think it's the best chance we have of controlling my brother and getting him to be cooperative."

"No, I mean why are you helping me at all? I know what I have to gain, but what's in it for you?"

"I'm repaying a long outstanding debt. My father took something from you, from both of us actually, and although my brother doesn't see it that way, I feel we owe you."

He seemed to soften by her words. "Your brother's right, it's not your debt to repay."

"Well, dead men can't make amends, so I guess you'll just have to deal with me."

He came and stood in front of her. "I am so grateful for everything you're doing for me, Monica. Thank you."

"Don't thank me yet, Congressman. So far I haven't achieved anything."

He put his hand on her shoulder. "I'm still grateful. The fact that you're even trying means a lot to me, and I won't forget it."

As was always the case with her, she wasn't comfortable with anyone touching her, but she decided to let it go as she reasoned she would need to tolerate this in front of people a little for the next few days, so needed to get used to it. "This won't be a spectator sport, Ryan. You will need to pull off a few Oscar winning performances yourself. You think you can handle that?"

He smiled. "I kiss babies for a living while they're dribbling all over me, and I'm telling their mothers how adorable they are. Trying to convince those around me that I find you sexually attractive is a walk in the park. You are a very desirable woman, Monica." His eyes ran up and down her body while his thumb started caressing her skin.

This was a bridge too far for Monica, so she took hold of his wrist and removed it from her shoulder. "Save it for when we have an audience, Congressman." She took a few steps away from him to give herself some distance. "Right, so first things first, I'm going to book us a table in one of our more romantic restaurants this evening. While we're there, I'll arrange to have all of your things moved to my personal quarters."

He was back to looking shocked again. "We're going to be sharing a bedroom?"

"Perish the thought." She made a little shudder. "I have spare rooms for my personal guests, so you will still have your privacy, but nobody needs to know that we will be sleeping alone."

He still looked uncertain. "Are you sure you know what you're doing, Monica?"

"Absolutely not; I haven't got a clue and am completely winging it, so just say the word and we will call the whole thing off. It's entirely up to you, Ryan, but decide now one way or another or if you have any better ideas, then please, tell me now, I'm all ears."

He remained silent.

She clapped her hands together. "Okay, then." She moved back towards the door. "Meet me in the garden bar at nine looking dazzlingly handsome and we will take it from there. We can strategize over dinner and get to know each other a little better. There are certain things that my brother would expect you to know if we were having regular sex."

He let out a deep breath. "Fine, we'll do this your way and let the cards fall where they may."

She took hold of his hand and shook it. "Here's to some successful bullshitting. Who knows, we may even have a little fun along the way."

He gave her a sexy smile. "That thought had occurred to me."

Chapter Five

      Monica had arranged for them to be seated at one of the corner alcoves. Intimate, with red velvet curtains draped all around them, illuminated only by candlelight, but with a shrouded open doorway making them easily seen for anyone that was looking.

The wine waiter approached them with a smile.

      "Ryan, how about some champagne, to celebrate you finally being here with me." She smiled subtly.

      He covered her hand that was lying on the table with his own. "Sounds perfect, darling."

      Monica physically resisted the shudder that wanted to run down her spine and kept the smile on her face. "A bottle of Cristal, please, Jeremy, and the usual for me."

He excused himself with a nod.

Monica looked down at her menu. "Don't overdo it, Congressman," she said through her teeth while pulling her hand out from under his.

"Too much?"

"Way too much. You have to remember that these people know me, and how I act, or more precisely, how I don't."

He put his menu down and looked at her. "But I don't, Monica, that's the point. You said act as though we're together, so in my mind that's what I did," he defended.

She looked at him. "Keep your voice down, and whatever you're saying to me, say it with a smile," she instructed.

He smiled tightly. "Yes, ma'am."

The waiter served their drinks.

When they were alone again, Ryan turned back to her. "So what is 'your usual' anyway?"

She picked up the glass flute in front of her. "Grape juice with tonic."

"You don't like champagne?"

"I don't drink."

"The receptionist told me that last night. How come? Was there a problem or something?"

Monica chuckled. "You mean because I'm a Katlyn, therefore, I must be an alcoholic? Play your cards right later,

Congressman, and I might show you the track marks left over from my heroin addiction days as well."

Ryan slowly closed his eyes and shook his head. "You're right; that was rude. I'm sorry."

She waved her hand dismissively at him as she continued to look down at the menu in front of her.

"Let me rephrase the question," he continued as he cleared his throat. "Why is it that you don't drink, Monica?"

She took a deep breath and looked at him again. "I have bad dreams when I drink."

"Every time?"

She nodded. "I don't know if it's because I'm allergic to it, or if I sleep too deeply, but either way, it doesn't agree with me."

"Do you only have the nightmares when you drink?"

She hesitated for a moment. "No. I suffer from them quite regularly, I always have, but they seemed to get worse when I drank, so I stopped."

"Are they different dreams, or the same recurring one, because if that's the case, it could be your subconscious trying to tell you something?"

She raised one side of her mouth. "Would you like me to lay down on a couch while we talk about this, and you can take notes? Be sure to tell me when my hour's up, though, won't you?"

He smiled. "Sorry. I've obviously spent way too much time in therapy myself."

"Well, it is the American way, isn't it? Practically your national pastime. Besides, you're right; you do need to know me a little better. Yes, it's the same dream, and no I don't want to talk about it, but that's irrelevant as it's not something my brother would know about to ask you."

She saw the waitress approaching in her peripheral vision so leant on one elbow and picked imaginary lint from his shoulder.

"Look at me adoringly, Congressman, but don't touch me."

He did as he was told. As the waitress walked through the curtained doorway, Monica cleared her throat and straightened in her chair as if she had been interrupted.

"Are you ready to order yet, Monica, or would you like a few more minutes to decide?"

"Sorry, Samantha, we got a little distracted. Could you bring us some oysters to start with please, while we finish making up our minds?"

She left them with a knowing smile.

Ryan chuckled. "You're very good at this, you know?"

"Presentation is what I do for a living, Ryan, and fortunately for you, you're right, I am very good at it."

"So you were about to start telling me a little about yourself?"

"Oh, goodie. Talking about myself, my favourite subject. You're going to have to bear with me on this, because letting people get to know me is *not* something I excel at."

"Why not just start from the beginning?" he suggested.

"No need, Nicky won't care about that."

"I care." He looked serious. "This isn't just about your brother, Monica; I'd genuinely like to take this opportunity to get to know you again."

She grinned. "I repeat, no need. I'm not exactly the caring and sharing type, Ryan, but let me tell you what you need to know. What Nicky will expect you to know."

The waitress returned with their oyster appetisers, and they both ordered then Monica waited until they were alone again before she continued.

"I know that you lost a parent all those years ago, but I lost both. From that night onwards I never spoke to my father again. Initially, because my aunt, my mother's sister, who took guardianship of me, wouldn't allow it, and then later, when I was old enough to understand what had really happened, because I didn't want to. I could never forgive my father for what he did, and I blame him for another death that night too; mine. The gangster's princess also died that night and 'she with the frozen heart' was created in her place, and that is who you see before you now."

"What does that mean?"

"Exactly what it sounds like I would imagine. I have two friends in the whole world, Wilhelmina, the night manager who you met last night, and Vincent, a guy that works for Nicky, who, if all goes well, you will meet at some point. Nobody else knows me because I don't allow them to."

"Why?"

"Because I won't allow myself to care enough for anyone to know me, and I certainly don't trust anyone enough. For most of my adult life, I've hidden who I truly am and that constant charade doesn't come without a price."

"Don't you get lonely?"

"I'm alone, but that's not the same thing as being lonely."

"So, you've never been involved with anybody, never been in love?"

"God, no." She did a dramatic shudder. "My only experience with love ended up in bloodshed, so why would I bother? Besides, I don't even like my body to be touched, let alone my heart."

"You don't like to be touched?" he said surprised.

Monica screwed her face up. "It kind of makes my skin crawl."

"So...does that mean...are you saying that...?"

"Spit it out, Ryan, I'm getting old over here."

"I'm sorry, it's just that it's probably a totally inappropriate question, but, are you telling me that you're a virgin?"

Monica burst out laughing. "Wow, Congressman, when you said it was an inappropriate question, I thought you were going to ask if I smoked or something," she teased.

He looked uncomfortable. "I'm sorry. Have I gone too far and asked you to overshare?"

"No, it's fine, and exactly the sort of thing my brother would expect you to know actually. I'm pretty much the furthest thing you can get from a virgin. I haven't been for a very long time."

"But you said you don't like to be touched."

"I don't like to be touched by other people, and certainly not without my express permission, but I don't have to be to enjoy sex, although sometimes I admit that I do allow a modicum of touching under certain circumstances if I'm in the right mood."

He looked confused.

"Let's just say I don't suppose for one moment that I have sex the way a governor's daughter does. Or maybe I'm wrong, what do I know about how you and Meredith get your naughty on? So how about it, Ryan, is there a lot of swinging from chandeliers in your love life?"

He grinned. "Not too much, no."

"I didn't think so. The point is, don't exaggerate things if you do meet with Nicky. He knows I have an active sex life, but he also knows that apart from the physical aspect, it has nothing to do with my feelings because I don't have any. I don't even tend to have sex with the same person twice."

"So how will he believe that we are in a relationship?"

"I said don't exaggerate, Ryan. If you use words like 'relationship' with regards to me, Nicky will laugh in your face. All we're trying to convince him of is that we're having regular sex, and my hope is that he will put it down to the fact that you were the first itch I had that I didn't get to scratch. You knew I had a crush on you when we were children, right?"

He grinned. "Yeah, I knew."

"Well, so did my brother and my hope is that he will think that's a good enough reason for me to have a little fascination with you, and why I believe we owe you a little payback."

"Okay, so what's the plan? How do we convince Nick that you are using me for my body but don't respect me in the mornings?"

She smiled. "Now you're getting it. To be honest, I have no idea. With my previous sexual partners, I barely remembered their names, and I'm not exactly big on the romance novels or anything, so I guess we just spend time together and hope the rest takes care of itself. You're going to need to clear your schedule for the next week or so. Is that going to be a problem?"

"It's a means to an end so I'll make it work somehow."

"And the white elephant that's not in the room? How are you going to placate your mother? Are you going to tell her what's going on?"

"No, there's no need. As you've intimated, my mother is one of my strongest allies in my political career and I'm grateful to her for the most part because she has always been there for me, but this is something I need to do on my own with as little outside involvement as possible. I'll think of something to explain my absence."

"You seriously think she doesn't know where you are right now, or won't find out? I think that very unlikely given what I remember of her, not to mention what I've read about the person she is now."

He shook his head. "There's no way she could know where I am. I told you, I didn't tell anybody I was coming, and I booked in here under an assumed name. A friend of mine that's out of the country and won't be back for a while."

"I know, I checked. I've deleted it completely from our system now, but if you want my advice, you'll make sure your mother is as oblivious as you think she is. It could throw a spanner in the works if she comes here, all guns blazing."

"It will be okay, trust me."

Monica smiled. "Not exactly a quick study are you, Congressman. I don't trust anyone, remember? But I will leave it with you as it's your political funeral if you're wrong."

He smiled. "If there's one thing I know how to do after all these years, its handle my mother. It won't be an issue; I assure you."

Chapter Six

Monica had been working for about three hours before Ryan entered her office the following morning.

He looked nervous. "I have been assured by your receptionist that I'm just allowed to walk in here, although I don't know who looked more shocked about it, her or me. I hope this is okay?"

"Of course, it's okay, Ryan." She waved her hand toward the door to indicate that he should shut it. Once completed she half smiled. "If you think she looked shocked when she relayed my instructions to you, you should have seen her face when she received them from me. I thought she was going to fall off her chair, bless her. Although to be fair I did tell her that you are free to come and go as you wish for as long as you stay with us, which is not something she has ever heard from me before."

"I take it not too many people are given a golden ticket to the chocolate factory then?"

"You would be the first, Charlie." She waved at the empty chair in front of her desk by way of an invitation. "So, how did you sleep?"

"Like a baby, although I don't know if that had more to do with the soft mattress and cool, crisp sheets or the champagne and brandies that I indulged in last night."

Monica shrugged. "Does it matter? Here, at Hotel Eden, so long as your every need is catered for, and you keep us just the right side of legal, we don't ever question the means. I'm sure a good night's sleep was just what the doctor ordered for you."

"Talking of which, did you even go to bed?"

"For a little while, yes. I don't tend to sleep for very long."

"Because of the night terrors, you told me about?" He looked concerned. "I've been thinking about what you said last night, and the more I do, the more I think I'm right. I really do think this recurring pattern is something psychosomatic, and a professional might be able to help you with it. Why don't you just look into it a little and maybe talk to someone?"

She smiled tightly. "Or perhaps I just accept the fact that I don't sleep for very long and deal with it accordingly."

"Why, what are you afraid of?"

She narrowed her gaze at him challengingly.

He held his hands up in surrender. "I apologise, that was a bad choice of words. What I mean is, if it is your mind's way of telling you something, wouldn't you rather know?"

She needed to end this particular topic of conversation as she was way out of her comfort zone. "I am an intelligent woman, Ryan. If my brain has decided to block something out, then I'm going to believe there was a definite reason for that, and if it's all the same to you, I'd rather not poke the bear. Now," she got to her feet, "have you had breakfast yet?"

He stood slowly and although he desperately wanted to push the matter, decided against it. "I had coffee in your apartment, but I wasn't sure whether I was supposed to eat up there or not?"

"I told you already, Congressman. Providing you don't get me arrested there are no rules at Hotel Eden, however, it might be a little remiss of you to have award winning chefs at your disposal and not take advantage of them, don't you think?"

He smiled. "I suppose it would, yes."

"Then let me accompany you. It seems like too nice a morning not to have breakfast on the sun patio, don't you think? That sounds to me like something two people having lots of regular sex might do."

"I think it might even be a law from where I come from," he teased.

She gave him a half grin. "Don't make fun of me. I told you I am completely winging it here and am so far out of my depth I can't even see the shoreline."

"You seem to be treading water just fine," he assured her as he extended his hand. "My lady," he said invitingly.

She looked at his hand then back at his face and shook her head. "Yeah, let's not overdo this."

She linked her arm through his and led the way, not releasing him until they were sat in the morning sunshine opposite each other. A waiter brought them coffee and took their orders.

Ryan looked around him appreciatively. "For fear of repeating myself and pissing you off again, this sure is one hell of a place you have here."

"Thank you. I must confess I am quite proud of it myself."

"As you should be, and I can understand the reclusiveness too. If I owned and worked in a place like this, I wouldn't want to leave it either. Hell, I don't think I'd even want to go inside."

"A bit of an outdoor kind of guy on the quiet, Congressman?"

"In another life I would think working outside, doing something with your hands, being at one with nature for want of a better word, would be a wonderful way to earn a living. A wonderful way to live."

"Not too much nature in the Capitol, I take it?"

He half smiled. "Plenty of wildlife, or should I say predators, but nature, no. You seem very happy in what you do. I envy you that."

"I take that to mean that you are not. If American politics isn't floating your boat anymore then why the need for another life? Do what makes you happy in this one."

"If only it were that simple."

"It is that simple, Ryan. It may not be easy, take it from someone who has spent years changing her destined path, but it is simple."

"Perhaps I lack the courage of your convictions. Not everybody is strong enough to go against their family like you did. Sometimes it's just easier to go with the flow."

"Please don't take this the wrong way but if you aren't strong enough to run your own family, how on earth do you think you are going to have what it takes to run a country some day? I will confess to knowing nothing of your world but surely to succeed in your chosen profession, you must have to have the drive, ambition and hunger to make that possible?"

He half smiled. "I guess that's the problem, it's not my chosen profession, but something that was chosen for me a very long time ago. You're right, though, you do have to want it, so that's why I'm surrounded by people that are hungry enough for me."

"Isn't that another way of basically saying that other people are running your life for you?"

"Of course, it is, because they are."

"And you say I need therapy," she said under her breath and took a mouthful of her coffee.

He smiled. "It's…complicated, Monica."

She looked serious. "It's not really, Ryan. It's your life, the only one you'll have, so man up and grow a pair and start living it."

"And how would you propose I do that?"

She half smiled. "Off the top of my head, I say you tell mommy dearest to shove it, resign from office, and I'll employ you as my head gardener. Problem solved."

He chuckled. "I'm not entirely sure that you're joking."

She raised an eyebrow. "Neither am I."

After breakfast Monica took Ryan on a tour of the house, pointing out all the more historical aspects, regaling him with all the scandals the property had suffered over the years and ending up in the clock tower, which practically overlooked the whole house.

Ryan leant against one of the stone arches and looked down at the building with all its architectural splendour. "It's breath-taking up here, Monica, truly spectacular."

"I come here quite often when I want to be alone, or if I have things on my mind, or if someone has completely pissed me off and I need to unwind." She smiled. "So you could say I'm up here most of the time really."

"I can see why. It's very...calming. I imagine you could stand here and let all this beauty take over you. I'm sure when it does you can convince yourself that anything is possible."

She smiled. "I thought this view might clinch it for you. Does that job offer seem a little more appealing right now?"

He turned his head to face her, his expression serious. "You have no idea how appealing all of this is to me but I don't think it's what destiny has in store for me. I got into politics because I truly believed I could make a difference, but it's so corrupt that sometimes it's almost impossible not to get caught up in all the bullshit. I want to help people and I'm sure that I can, given the chance, but it's whether I can do that without selling my soul, that's the problem."

She half shrugged. "Destiny is just a word, Ryan, and in itself, not so scary. Think of it like a train. If you don't like where yours is heading, then change your ticket."

"And what about your ticket? Is this the end of the line for you now, are you done?"

She slowly shook her head as she sat down on one of the stone benches. "I'll never be done. I'm like a shark, if I stop swimming, I die. Eden will be spreading its wings soon enough and I'll be adding a sister hotel to the family, I just need to decide where to go?"

He came and sat beside her. "You really are in control of your own destiny now, aren't you?"

"I changed my ticket a long time ago, Congressman."

"Does anything scare you? Have you ever once been faced with a challenge that you didn't meet head on and just walked away?"

"Don't for one minute think of me as the poster child for normal living, Ryan. I have so many hang ups you'd need a calculator to count them, I just work around them, that's all. Fear isn't a bad thing you know. Without fear, we wouldn't ever have the opportunity to be brave. Walking a tightrope isn't brave if you're not afraid of it, it's just walking a tightrope."

"I find your simplistic view on life very refreshing. Does it come in a bottle by any chance?" He smiled.

"It's far too potent for that, and you should be careful because it can very quickly become addictive."

"I don't doubt it for a moment."

Monica got to her feet. "Do you ride, Congressman?"

"I do. Why, what did you have in mind?"

"Well, you've seen the house, now let's go and see the grounds the way they should be seen, on horseback. I guarantee you, you'll never want to set foot in another limo again."

He smiled. "Lead the way, ticket master."

After three hours of riding the grounds and showing Ryan what she considered being the most beautiful areas of her property, Monica slowed to a gentle trot and Ryan came up alongside her.

She looked at him with a smile. "You should stick with your instincts, Congressman; the outdoors seems to agree with you."

He breathed out a laugh. "This place...it's just...amazing. A man could get used to living like this; that's for sure."

"Ready to give up all the glamour of Washington so soon? Tut, tut, Congressman, what would your mother say?"

His face turned serious. "You make me feel as though I almost want to find out."

"Only almost? Then my work here is obviously not yet done," she teased. "Hungry?"

"I could eat, but isn't the house back the other way?"

"The main house is, but that's not where we're having lunch. I have smaller cottages dotted all over the grounds for those guests that desire a more romantic setting for a weekend getaway or just a little more privacy."

"And which are we?" He smiled.

"As far as the outside world is concerned, we're both."

"And as far as we're concerned?"

She smiled. "Don't flirt with me, Congressman. Trust me; you'd be biting off more than you could chew."

"I told you I could eat," he joked.

They arrived at the cottage; tied, fed and watered the horses and then walked around the front of the house. Their lunch lay covered under a gazebo, and a huge blanket lay beside it on the floor covered in throw pillows.

"Wow, a picnic! This is fantastic," he beamed.

"I'm glad you approve. Come on, let me show you the inside of the house so you can say that you've seen it if, by some chance, it comes up in conversation with my brother."

She showed him all around the luxury home ending in the bedroom with the king-size bed draped in white silk; the curtains pulled closed and the whole room filled with candles.

"You arranged all of this?" he asked quietly.

"I did. We want everyone to think I brought you out here to seduce you, remember?"

He turned to face her. "Are you going to seduce me?"

"I don't seduce anyone, Ryan; I have sex. This..." she waved her hand in the air to indicate the room, "this is just what I do to keep the guests happy. It's not real, and it's certainly not me."

"What is you?"

She took a step towards him, looking him straight in the eye. "Hard, heavy, sweaty, completely carnal and in absolute control, with my partner's total surrender. That's me."

He licked his suddenly dry lips. "You make it sound almost scary?"

She gave him half a smile. "Only when I do it right. Come on." She turned away from him. "Let's go and get something to eat. Remind me before we leave, to mess up those sheets a little."

He grabbed her wrist. "Why don't we mess them up now, together?" he teased.

She looked over her shoulder at him. "You can either let me have sex with you, Ryan, or you can let me try to be your friend. You can't have both. You need me far more as a friend right now than you need your next orgasm, and I think you know that."

"Why can't I have both?"

"It doesn't work that way with me, Congressman; I don't know how to do both. I did mention that I have certain hang-ups, right?"

"It may have come up," he conceded.

"Then you would do well to bear that in mind. Now let's go and eat and I'll try my best to forget the fact that you are touching me right now without my express permission."

He half smiled then his face dropped, and he released her wrist. "My God, you're serious?"

"I usually am. Don't worry about it, Ryan; I have no problem reminding you of the rules until they sink in."

She led him back outside where they helped themselves to food then settled on the ground propped up by pillows.

Ryan situated himself as far away from her as he could while still remaining on the blanket.

She looked at him and chuckled. "You don't have to be so nervous around me now, you know, I don't bite. Well…actually, I do sometimes, but I won't be biting you today so you can relax."

He smiled. "I don't want to do the wrong thing inadvertently and not know it. You are a very difficult person to read sometimes."

"Actually, I'm not; you just don't have to overcomplicate things. Listen to what I tell you, and I mean, really listen, and everything will be fine. I will never tell you anything that isn't true, nor will I say something because I think it's what you want to hear. It doesn't get any simpler than that."

"And you've always been this way?"

She half shrugged. "As far back as I can really remember. I have a lot of blank spots from my childhood, and I try not to focus on them too much. I accept the fact that I'm broken and live my life accordingly."

"I don't think you're broken. A little unusual perhaps, but that isn't necessarily a bad thing. If anything, I think it's quite refreshing actually."

She smirked. "Unusual is probably the nicest way I've ever been described, thank you for that, Ryan."

He smiled. "You're very welcome." He rolled onto his side and leant his head on his elbow. "Tell me why you think you're broken?"

She put the plate she was holding to one side and reached behind her to open the wine that was waiting in the ice bucket. She poured him a glass then turned to face him.

"Don't assume that I think being broken is necessarily a bad thing. If I weren't broken, then I would have continued my family tradition of becoming a fully-fledged member of Murder Incorporated as soon as I hit puberty. My defects enabled me to make a different choice although it doesn't come without a price. I'd be the first to admit that I haven't got very much of a clue as to how normal people feel, but I know enough to know that I'm practically dead inside. For the most part, I feel absolutely nothing. That's not me attempting to throw myself a pity party; it's just the way I feel. Even I know that's not right, but it is what it is, and there is nothing I can do about it, even if I wanted to, which, for the most part, I don't."

He took a mouthful of his wine while contemplating her words. "I struggle to understand how somebody who claims to be dead inside can make me feel so alive."

"That's not me making you feel that way; it's this place. Hotel Eden has magical qualities, you know."

"Is that right?"

She nodded. "Absolutely. That's how I get away with charging the outrageous prices that I do, because of the magic."

He smiled. "Worth every dime."

He was quiet for a few moments while he sipped his wine and took in their surroundings.

"Do you ever wonder what could have happened between us if I'd remained in England after that night, or indeed if that night had never happened?" he asked without facing her.

She rolled onto her stomach and started picking at the grass. "I used to. More precisely, I used to imagine you coming back for me. You would swoop back into my life to save me, and we would ride off into the sunset together and live happily ever after." She chuckled.

He turned his head to face her. "I'm here now."

"But now I'm way past saving."

"And your childhood crush has long since passed and you don't want me anymore?"

"Of course, I do, as much as I want anyone. I appreciate beauty, Ryan, in whatever form, and you are one of the beautiful people. However, I want to help you more than I want to have sex with you. I think if I do this, it might make me feel better about myself."

"How?"

"I don't know. I just feel as far back as I can remember I'm carrying around this tremendous feeling of guilt that seems to shadow everything else. My hope is that I feel guilty about what my father did to your family and by helping you now, it might alleviate that somehow. Perhaps, by helping you get to the White House, I might find a little redemption in that."

"You shouldn't feel guilty for other people's actions. You had no control over what your father did."

"I'm aware of that, and I know it's crazy, but whenever I think back to that night, I always have this overwhelming burst of guilt come over me, like somehow it was my fault and I should have done something differently, which I know is ridiculous as I was only a child and my father was the true villain of the story but I can't help how I feel."

"Neither can I. I'm what you would call a rare breed in Washington, not only for my single-mindedness in always wanting to be my own man but also in that, whenever possible I tend to be honest, so I think it only fair to tell you that I'm starting to feel very drawn to you, Monica. I'm beginning to have trouble controlling my actions around you, and I think the more time I spend with you, the harder it's going to get."

"If it helps at all, you could just keep telling yourself that if you act inappropriately, I might be tempted to kick your arse." She smiled.

"I'm not sure that it does, but I'll try to bear it in mind. Are we spending the night here?"

She shook her head. "No, but when we return to the house, we'll take the backstairs by the clock tower because there are no cameras there, so everyone will think that we have stayed here. It's my little escape route when I don't want anyone to know about my comings or goings."

"Why pretend? Surely it would be easier just to stay here?"

"There's only one bed."

He grinned. "Don't tell me that you're that much of a prude that you couldn't share a bed with me?"

She half laughed. "Hardly a prude, Ryan, but when I sleep, I have to sleep alone."

"Another one of your eccentricities?"

She grinned. "Now you're starting to get me, Congressman."

"Perhaps, but maybe it will be too little, too late, unless of course you're thinking that any of those sister hotels you were telling me about are going to be Stateside? I can't help but think I have been given a second chance to have you back in my life, and I'm not sure I'm ready to give that up."

"No, I have more tropical climates in mind for my next venture. Besides, if we manage to pull off our little ruse, I will be very much persona non grata as far as your constituents would be concerned."

He took in a deep breath and rolled onto his back. "Ah, yes, we mustn't forget about the constituents, must we? Heaven forbid I ever decide something for myself based on what I want, as opposed to always being seen to do the right thing." He closed his eyes. "God, I am so tired of all the bullshit."

"What is it that you think you want, Ryan?"

He turned his head slightly to look at her. "Right now, I want you."

"You don't know me, Ryan, so you can't possibly fathom what it is you're asking for."

"Educate me."

She rolled her eyes. "You're not going to let this go, are you?"

"Only if I have to. You need to explain to me why would it be so wrong for the two of us to become…involved?"

"Just trust me, Ryan, it would, for so many reasons, none of which you will probably understand."

"So, explain them to me then?"

"No, it will be quicker and easier if I just placate you."

"Meaning?"

"Meaning, unbutton your shirt."

He raised his eyebrows. "Excuse me?"

"I think you heard me, Ryan, unbutton your shirt. I'm going to give you a taste of what it is you think you want."

He hesitated for a moment before his hands went to the first button on his shirt and he started slowly undoing them, never taking his eyes from hers.

"Now, undo your belt, and then your jeans," she instructed.

"Aren't we going to take this inside?"

"No, we're not, now do as I ask."

"But…somebody could come along and see us?"

"You're right, they could; now do as I say right now, or don't because I won't ask you again."

He swallowed deeply then complied.

She sidled closer to him and ran her fingernails down his chest and into the top of his pubic hair. "Show me what you've got, Congressman."

His breathing had gotten heavy. "Help yourself."

"It doesn't work that way, Ryan. I want you to show me. I want to see you touching yourself."

"Why?" he breathed.

"Because I like it. This isn't about emasculating you; it's about the fact that you say I turn you on, and you are going to return the favour now and let me see you touch yourself."

He slowly slid his hand into his jeans and pulled out his now erect penis, looking at her for further instructions.

She smiled. "That's holding, Ryan, not touching, and I'm sure you can do better than that. You know what I want to see, so do it."

"I'd much rather you do it," he almost pleaded.

"I'm sure you would, but that doesn't work for me." She circled his nipple with her index finger. "Come for me, Congressman."

He started stroking himself, tentatively at first, until Monica ran her fingernails down his ribs and he tightened his grip as his wrist seemed to take on a mind of its own, which he was unsure how to cope with, having never felt quite like this before.

"Just let go, Ryan," she whispered into his ear. "Give in to that overall feeling of pleasure that's waiting to spring from you. There is no right or wrong here, there's just you, touching yourself for me, and it feels so good, doesn't it, you know that it does."

His breath was coming in gasps now as he increased his pace.

"Do it, Ryan, do it for me. I want to see you come for me; you have no idea how much I want to see that, do it for me, do it for me now."

He cried out as he ejaculated all over himself. Monica sat up and watched him while his breathing returned to normal then he turned to face her.

"What now?" he said expectantly.

She shrugged. "Now, I would suggest that you go inside and clean yourself up, but that's just me."

He drew his eyebrows together. "You mean we're done? What about your turn?"

"That was never about me, Ryan; it was about trying to help you keep your libido in check."

He chuckled. "That has never been a problem for me until now. What are you doing to me, Monica? The way you make me feel, the things you make me do, what's happening to me?"

She smiled. "I told you, it's magic."

He joined her smile. "I think that it is."

He got up and went to the bathroom while she checked her phone for messages. When he joined her again, one look at her face told him she wasn't happy.

"Problems?" he asked.

"Potentially, for you," she said flatly. "Do you remember me saying to you that you needed to take care of your mother because it could quite dramatically fuck things up if she got involved and you said you'd handle it?"

"I do and I did. I couldn't get hold of her, but I left her a message to say I was taking a few days off and would speak to her next week when I got back. It will be fine; I assure you."

She smiled tartly. "Yeah, not so much. I've just been paged to say there is an Annabel Whittaker waiting at the house and is very insistent on seeing me. A coincidence you think? Maybe she was just in the neighbourhood and thought she would stop by for a catch-up?"

He closed his eyes and let out a deep breath. "Fuck," he said to himself.

"Fuck, indeed, Congressman," Monica concurred, and she got to her feet. "You need to make her stand down, Ryan. Things are precarious enough as it is, without her interfering."

"I'll take care of it, I promise."

Monica looked unconvinced. "And I promise, if you don't, I will."

Chapter Seven

When they finally arrived back at the main house after stabling the horses, Monica gave Ryan a few minutes head start with his mother while she freshened up then she joined them in one of the many lounges. At this time of the day, it was busy with afternoon teas, and she momentarily worried about the potential scene that could very well be about to happen. One look at Annabel Whittaker's face told Monica it was practically a foregone conclusion. Perhaps it was for the best she reasoned, as if anything was going to be fed back to her brother's ears, a public showdown with her so-called lover's mother, in front of other paying guests, would certainly make the list.

She approached the sofas they were sat on with a smile.

Ryan got to his feet. "Mother, allow me to reintroduce you to Monica Maxwell. Monica, you remember my Mother, Annabel Whittaker."

Annabel more touched Monica's hand than shook it and the contact was incredibly brief.

She looked older than Monica remembered, understandably so, but also harder. She was immaculately presented but carried an air about her as though the entire world continually disappointed her. For reasons Monica could not understand she felt a sudden sense of revulsion come over her in this woman's presence, and she physically had to swallow the lump in her throat that she could only describe as fear running through her. Both feelings were as alien as they were unexpected and she momentarily panicked that she would not be able to handle this woman, that she somehow posed too big of a threat to be denied.

"Monica Maxwell, indeed," Annabel sneered. "It is good of you to join us, finally. I trust I didn't drag you away from anything too important?"

The dismissive tone she used and the insinuation that she was not happy to have been kept waiting was not lost on Monica and was exactly what she needed to get her back on an even keel.

"Nothing that couldn't wait, which I would have thought was obvious by my presence now," Monica replied with an abundantly clear false smile.

The rise to Annabel Whittaker's eyebrow told Monica her retort had hit its target.

"Perhaps it would be for the best if you left *Monica* and me alone for a while, Ryan?" Annabel informed her son.

"That's not going to happen, Mother, I'm staying," he replied flatly.

She went to contradict him, but he interrupted her.

"I said I'm staying, now say what it is you feel you need to say to Monica and then allow us to carry on with the rest of our day."

Monica fought to hide the grin she was feeling at the look on Annabel's face, obviously not used to being spoken to like that by her son, and was blatantly surprised by it.

She composed herself quickly and turned back to Monica. "I suppose I should apologise for turning up here unannounced as I have although I can hardly believe that my arrival here is a surprise."

"Turning up unannounced seems to be something of a family trait, and as for it being a surprise..." Monica glanced at Ryan, "let's just say it is to some more than others," she said knowingly, as she sat down on the opposite sofa facing them. "The last time I saw you I referred to you as Aunt Anna. I suppose that would no longer be appropriate?" she teased.

"No, it would not," Annabel snapped, seemingly displeased at Monica's attempt at joviality. "I am doing my best to be civil, but please do not expect anything more than that from me as I have had a very long journey, I am tired and most unhappy at having to be here at all."

Monica raised her eyebrows. "How unfortunate for you, and please don't feel the need for civility on my account. So, Mrs Whittaker it is then. Tell me, Mrs Whittaker; my staff informed me that you were asking to see me, quite insistently apparently, so how exactly can I help you today?"

Annabel glared at her. "Is that supposed to be some kind of a joke, young lady?"

"Not at all, I assure you. I assume you didn't come all this way just to catch up or to see how I am, so you are going to have to explain to me what possible business you and I would have to discuss."

Annabel took a deep breath as if mentally counting to ten. "I came to inform my son that for the sake of his political career, his little sabbatical is over, and he needs to come home with me right now."

Monica glanced at Ryan, who was sat back with his legs crossed and looking out the window, attempting it seemed to ignore his mother's presence completely.

"I see. And what exactly does that have to do with me?"

"Don't play games with me, Rebecca Katlyn, or whatever it is you're calling yourself these days. You know very well what it has to do with you, now give my son the assurances that he so ill-advisedly came here for personally, and then we will be on our way."

"What assurances are those?"

"That you will not cause any problems when approached about the past, and then we will go and that will be an end to it."

"Perhaps Ryan has not had the opportunity to explain to you that he already has my assurances in that matter unreservedly and that his extended stay here is just to secure the same from my brother, who is perhaps not quite as amenable as I am. I assure you I am in no way forcing Ryan to remain here against his will, Mrs Whittaker; I am merely taking advantage of the fact that he is here, to get…re-acquainted."

"That re-acquaintance is exactly my problem and could potentially be his downfall. I won't stand for it."

Monica raised one side of her mouth. "What exactly do you propose to do about it; ground him?"

"I'll thank you not to adopt that tone with me, young lady, as my patience is understandably running very thin at the moment, and you really don't want to see my bad side."

Monica smiled. "Who says I don't want to see that, Mrs Whittaker. I'll show you mine if you show me yours."

Annabel turned to her son. "Ryan, I am obviously wasting my time here."

"You're wasting all of our time, Mother. You should never have come here in the first place. This is my business and I will take care of it. How did you even know I was here?"

The slight blush to Annabel's face told Ryan all he needed to know.

"Oh, my God, she's right. You do have me followed, don't you?" he said accusingly.

"I do what is necessary to protect you, Ryan, and I always will."

Ryan sat up straight in his seat. "Have a care, Mother. I've always appreciated your support throughout my life, but remember, it is *my* life, and while support will be tolerated, interference will not."

"Anything I do is always with your best interests at heart. You need to leave with me now and let me take care of everything. I know how to handle the Katlyn's, I always have."

Monica chuckled. "And how exactly do you propose to do that? I'm hoping that charm isn't your plan A, because if that's the case, then your son is well and truly screwed."

Annabel faced her again. "Since when would charm work on the likes of you? You and your entire family have always been, and will always be, two steps away from pure white trash."

Monica half smiled. "Probably closer to one step away in all honesty, but who's counting and what exactly is your point?"

"My point is that you swan around here in your fancy hotel, mixing with the best your society has to offer and pretending that you're one of them, but we both know you're not, and you never will be. How well do you think your business would fair if I decided to tell everyone just who in fact you are?"

"Don't threaten her, Mother, because the situation may not be as it appears and I will warn you again not to interfere."

Monica looked at Ryan. "She hasn't got the slightest clue what's going on, has she?"

"She hasn't given me much of an opportunity to explain it to her," he snapped, all aggression clearly directed towards his mother.

Monica edged forward in her seat. "Annabel," she smiled sarcastically, "and yes, I am going to use your first name because, after today, you and I will never be seeing each other again, but while I have you in front of me, let me educate you a little about my business. I own one of the most prestigious hotels this country has ever seen. My society, as you so glibly put it, or more accurately, my guest list of regular clients, is a veritable who's who from all over the world. Have you met the current President, by any chance, because I have? The waiting list alone to get in here dictates when many people take their trips as they don't wish to stay anywhere else, and do you know what would happen if people found out who I really was, what *will* happen, in fact, because I have every intention of revealing myself on behalf of your son; my business will increase tenfold. Unlike that of your son's, there is no such thing in my business as bad publicity, my scandalous past, or more accurately my family's past would merely pull in a larger crowd. I have kept my anonymity all these years because I felt it was my own personal business, not because I thought for one moment that it would have an adverse effect on me professionally. I have now accepted the fact that in assisting your son I will be coming out of the proverbial closet, and I will handle it accordingly. You are in my corner of the world right now, Annabel. I have money, power and connections, all in abundance, so don't think for one moment that you can come waltzing in here in your last season's Chanel suit and make me nervous, because you can't."

A red-faced Annabel turned towards her son. "Are you just going to sit there and let her talk to me that way, Ryan?"

His expression seemed bored. "And what exactly would you like me to do? You rolled the dice, Mother. I warned you to stay out of this and not interfere, but you wouldn't listen."

"How can I not interfere when I see you making such a monstrous mistake as this? What did you have to promise her precisely in order to obtain her cooperation?"

"Mother, that's enough!" he barked. "Monica has bent over backwards to help me, and still is in point of fact, and I will not repay that kindness by sitting here and allowing you to insinuate it was for anything other than out of the goodness of her heart."

Annabel looked back at Monica apparently unconvinced. "The goodness of her heart, indeed," she said to herself. "My son seems to be quite taken in by you, *Monica*. Tell me, what possible leverage do you imagine that your brother could have against my son that would justify our compliance in this matter and have him jumping through hoops the way you have?"

"Leverage on your son, none, to the best of my knowledge. You, however, are quite a different story."

"Me? What could you possibly mean by that? I don't have the faintest idea to what you could be referring to."

"I think you do. You keep insinuating that my life is a lie when in fact it's yours that is. Annabel Whittaker may think she is whiter than white, but perhaps she doesn't remember Annabel Montgomery quite as well as I do, or more importantly, as well as my brother does."

Annabel pulled back slightly and swallowed deeply. "Whatever lies your brother is inclined to tell about my previous association with your family would be nothing more than hearsay and would be dealt with accordingly," she said uncertainly.

"It's not hearsay, Mother," Ryan interjected. "Apparently you have gone on the record a number of times stating you barely knew Monica's family, particularly her father, and had very little interaction with them. Her brother has photographic evidence to dispute that, some of which it would seem is of such a delicate nature it could hurt us substantially."

"Like what, for instance?" she persisted.

"Like taking drugs for a start. We can't risk something like that getting out, Mother, it would ruin me."

Annabel remained silently indignant while seeming to contemplate Ryan's words and the implications of them.

"It would appear Ryan's acquaintance with *you* is potentially his greatest downfall, don't you think, Annabel? Oh, the irony is just so…delicious." Monica smiled, unable to resist the opportunity to turn the tables.

Annabel cleared her throat and ran her hand across her lap removing imaginary creases. "So, it's blackmail then? And…if such proof exists, and I'm not saying that it does, how much would it take to make sure it didn't ever see the light of day?"

Monica slowly shook her head in disbelief. "You just don't get it, do you? Both my brother and I could buy and sell you many times over. Nicky isn't interested in your money; he has plenty of his own, he much prefers to keep adding to his personal collection by owning people, and I'm trying desperately hard to avoid that if at all possible."

"And how exactly do you propose to do that? Am I supposed to believe that he too is going to assist Ryan out of the goodness of his heart," she said sarcastically.

"Only if you are more stupid than you look, which, with some of the comments that have come out of your mouth this afternoon, I haven't completely ruled out yet as a distinct possibility."

A red-faced Annabel ignored that insult. "Explain it to me then?" she said demandingly.

Monica took a deep breath and looked at Annabel as if addressing a child. "I have asked my brother to comply as a personal favour to me because of mine and Ryan's…association."

"And will he?"

"I hope so, but there are certainly no guarantees at this stage," Monica replied honestly.

Annabel turned to Ryan. "You are going to risk the rest of your entire career on hope? Are you really happy to do that given everything that is at stake here, Ryan?"

"It's my best option, Mother, so I will ask you again, in fact, no, I'm telling you, do not interfere and let Monica and myself handle this."

"It is most certainly not your best option; you have just been brainwashed into thinking that it is." She turned back to Monica. "Are you also sleeping with my son, *Monica*?"

Ryan went to speak, but Annabel raised a hand to stop him.

"I want to hear this from her, Ryan, and don't think for one moment that she is too delicate to respond, as she is, after all, her mother's daughter."

The challenge in the other woman's voice was too much for Monica to ignore.

Monica licked her lips, not trying to hide the amusement she was feeling at her opponent's frustrations. "Is that important, Annabel. Am I not daughter-in-law material in your mind?"

"Answer my question," Annabel snapped.

"For me to answer that question, Annabel, it would infer that it is acceptable for you to have asked it, and it most certainly is not. Whatever is or is not happening between Ryan and myself, is, well, quite frankly, none of your business."

"If my son has been manipulated enough to commit political suicide, it is very much my business."

"As point of fact, it's not, but for some reason Ryan has indulged you so much over the years that you have convinced yourself that it is."

Annabel glanced and Ryan and then back at Monica. "You do realise that he already has a woman in his life, a respectable woman, far more suited to his station?"

Monica nodded. "I do."

"And that doesn't bother you at all, does it?" she stammered. "You are still quite happy to carry on your illicit affair without a care in the world. Well, this apple obviously didn't fall too far from the tree because you are every bit the whore your mother was."

"That's enough!" Ryan snapped.

Monica held up a hand to silence him as she edged slightly closer to his mother. "Let me tell you what's about to happen now, Annabel. Within the next few minutes you are going to leave my property, and that is an unequivocal fact. What is still somewhat up for debate is how you leave, be it of your own volition, or…how shall I put this…with assistance. One more word from you about my mother and you will be escorted from these premises. Oh, and just to make sure you appreciate my meaning, by escorted I do of course mean frogmarched with a man on each arm, and not in a good way, and by premises I do of course mean dropped on your tight little arse at the main outer entrance. Just so you know, although I never let paparazzi on the grounds, you will always find them at the gate. Wouldn't it be a shame if such an embarrassing exit from my hotel were to be photographed, and then they somehow got an anonymous tip telling them exactly who you were and giving them your name, Mrs Annabel Whittaker?"

Annabel glared at her. "You wouldn't dare," she challenged.

Monica smiled. "That's an incredibly stupid thing to say to a Katlyn, especially given the fact that for some reason, I seem to be feeling an instant and almost overpowering dislike of you, Mrs Whittaker, which is unusual for me to say the least as most people don't even really register on my radar emotionally, so I guess my reply to you, given all those facts, is…try me, bitch."

Annabel looked at Ryan to intervene.

He got to his feet and gently took her elbow. "Come along, Mother, I'll walk you out."

Her mouth fell open in astonishment. "You can't be serious? Surely you aren't going to allow this woman to control you like this and just take it? Have you lost your mind?"

"I'm doing what I always do, Mother, what you taught me to do ever since I entered the world of politics, and that's to surround myself with the best advisors. Given the subject matter, I believe Monica to be the best advisor."

She reluctantly got to her feet while picking up her bag and turned back to Monica. "It appears I underestimated you, *Monica*. Enjoy the feeling while it lasts because that won't happen again the next time we meet, I assure you. This is by no means over."

Monica stood with a smile. "Let us hope for both our sakes that you're wrong and there isn't a next time for us. I may not be as inclined to play quite so nicely again." She turned to Ryan. "I'll meet you upstairs once you've seen your mother out."

As she turned to walk away, Annabel stopped her wanting to have the final word.

"So eager to get him alone again so you can fill his head with even more of your lies. It's good to see that I have at the very least unnerved you," she said smugly.

Monica took a step closer to whisper in her ear. "I'm not taking him upstairs to *talk* to him, Annabel. Why don't you think about all of the disgusting things I am about to do to your son while you're travelling home without him." She pulled back and winked at her.

A red-faced Annabel glared at her. "I say again, every bit the whore your mother was!" she uncharacteristically screamed, any pretence of control well and truly gone.

The whole room fell silent after sharp intakes of breaths all around and with all eyes now on them, it turned an angry Annabel Whittaker into a mortified one as she realised the spectacle she had just made of herself.

Monica grinned. "Thank you for that, because now it means I can do this." She pulled her phone out of her back pocket and pressed a button. "Send security to the blue lounge immediately, please. I need an extraction to be taken all the way to the front gate."

Ryan was the first to react. "You're leaving right now, Mother, before this does end up in the papers."

He practically dragged her from the room spitting and spluttering, and Monica smiled to herself as she put her dormant phone back into her pocket having not spoken with anyone.

By the time Ryan returned to her apartment, she was sat at her desk going through some paperwork. She looked up in greeting and he had a very subservient look on his face.

"Monica, I owe you an apology, I'm sorry, I had no idea she would do anything like that."

"You don't owe me an apology for that, Ryan; it was…fun. What you do owe me is a 'you were right and I was wrong, Monica,' and I owe you an 'I told you so, Ryan'," she said assuredly, amusement still very evident on her face.

He slowly smiled and slightly bowed his head. "You were right, and I was wrong, Monica."

"I told you so, Ryan," she said smugly and grinned.

He took a step closer to her. "I have never seen her lose control like that before. I've got to ask. What on earth did you say to her to warrant such a response?"

She looked back down at the paperwork in front of her. "I insinuated to her that I was going to be having sex with you this afternoon," she said casually, as though she were talking about the weather.

He chuckled. "So, you lied?"

She signed her name to the document she had just finished reading, put her pen down then sat back in her chair looking at his face again. "That depends on you I suppose so why don't you tell me, did I lie?"

His face lost all expression. "Are you…are you saying you want to have sex with me?"

"Yes," she said flatly.

He contemplated her answer for a moment. "Is…is that because of my mother?"

"Yes."

He huffed out a breath. "Well, don't sugar-coat it for me or anything will you, it might go to my head?"

"Ryan, you need to stop thinking of things in the way of ego, or emotion, because that's not what we're talking about. All that would be between us would be mutual physical gratification, and nothing more. Just sex in its most basic form. We won't be making sweet, sweet love then lying in each other's arms while we pillow talk our way through our hopes and dreams. Just sex, take it or leave it, but understand fully, that it will change nothing between us."

He looked unsure whether to be insulted or not. "And all of this is because of my mother?" he repeated.

"To be absolutely honest there's a part of it that's a 'fuck you' to Annabel Whittaker, but there is also the part that I told you about earlier, which is I appreciate beauty and you are certainly very easy on the eyes, Congressman. Combine the two and I seem to have run out of good enough reasons *not* to do this. So I will ask you again, did I lie when I insinuated to your mother that we will be having sex this afternoon?"

"I don't have the faintest idea what I'm getting into here, but I have a very strong feeling that I would never forgive myself if I didn't at least try to see it through, so...so no, you didn't lie."

He knelt down beside her and turned her chair slightly towards him while he started moving his face closer to hers.

She pulled back from him. "What are you doing, Ryan?"

He drew his eyebrows together. "Are you saying that we can make lo…, sorry, that we can have sex, but we can't kiss?"

"Why on earth would we want to? Sex has a purpose, kissing on the mouth in my mind does not and it just always seems so pointless to me. Don't misunderstand me, I have nothing against using my tongue, or you using yours for that matter, but there are much better ways to use it than kissing I assure you."

He looked almost amused. "What if I like kissing?"

"Then I'm very happy for you, and hope for your sake that Meredith does too, then that way, you can save them all for her."

He breathed out a laugh. "I think you mean that."

"With all of my..." she smiled, and half shrugged, "well, perhaps heart is the wrong word, but you get the idea."

"What I don't have an idea about is what to do next? I...I don't know what you expect from me." He chuckled. "I feel like that awkward teenager that I was again, on my first date, without a clue of what I'm doing."

She raised one side of her mouth. "That doesn't sound like a happy memory for you, Ryan?"

He grimaced. "No, it's not particularly. I was so clumsy that I hurt her lip with my teeth, so she didn't even let me get to second base. To add insult to injury, she told the entire school about it."

Monica chuckled. "Wow, that I agree doesn't sound like a happy memory. Let's see if we can improve on that the second time around. If it makes you feel better, you are guaranteed to get way beyond second base today, I have no problem with you using your teeth, and I won't be telling anybody anything."

"Now, that does make me feel better. Where were you when I needed you at my high school reunion?" He smiled.

"That's better; that smile. Just try to relax and remember this is all about enjoyment and nothing else otherwise there's no point."

She took his hand as she got to her feet then led him into the bedroom he was staying in.

She turned to face him beside the bed. "Don't be scared and if I do anything you don't like, or you want me to stop, just say the word and I'll stop."

He looked dubious. "Has that ever happened to you before? Has anyone ever really asked you to stop?"

She half smiled. "I work on the theory that there's always a first time for everything."

"I don't think today is going to be the day for that particular first, Monica. I don't know where this is going, but wherever it leads, I'm in, all the way."

"Let's see about that, shall we?"

Her hands went to the first button on his shirt. He raised his own hands to mirror her actions, but she slowly shook her head, so he lowered them again. When she had undone all of the buttons, she walked behind him, reaching over his shoulders to pull on his shirt, so it slid down his back.

She let go of the shirt so it fell to the floor and the exposed skin that was now in front of her she ran fingernails down. He did an involuntary shiver.

Monica chuckled. "A little bit ticklish, are we, Congressman?"

His breathing was starting to get heavier. "Either that or I'm just scared shitless."

She put her mouth to his ear. "Fear has no place in this room right now, Ryan," she whispered as she ran her fingernails around his ribs, bringing her hands up to circle his nipples lightly.

He took in a deep, steadying breath. "I thought that you said you didn't like touching?"

"What I said was I don't like to be touched. I have nothing at all against touching." She ran her hands down his abdomen. "In fact, I would go so far as to say," she ran a hand around his belly button and then both hands started running along the top of his jeans, "that the only thing better than looking at beauty," she slipped her fingertips under his waistband, "is touching it, and the only thing better than touching it," she pulled her hands back up and started undoing his belt, "is tasting it." She gently nipped his earlobe with her front teeth.

"I very much think I'm going to approve of the way you appreciate beauty," he breathed.

"Now you're getting it," she whispered as she pulled back and ran her lips across his shoulder blade. "It's all about what we like," she said against his skin. "It's all about what feels good, and enjoying each other."

She pulled back from him, so he went to turn, but she put her hands on his arms to stay him.

"Don't move, Ryan, I want you exactly where you are, for now."

She pulled her t-shirt over her head and unhooked her bra letting it fall to the floor at his feet. Bracing her hands on his hips, she rubbed her nipples against his bare back, then keeping him close, her hands went back to the front of his jeans. She slowly unbuckled his belt and as the zip went down, her right hand followed suit and slipped inside his boxer shorts, taking hold of his penis.

He exhaled loudly with a jolt. "Oh, yes, now that's what I'm talking about," he breathed.

She smiled against his spine. "If that's *all* you're talking about then you definitely do need to broaden your horizons."

"Please, feel free to educate me," he almost pleaded.

"I do, and I will," she assured him.

She stroked him firmly while pushing down his jeans with her other hand. As they slipped to his knees, she released him and ran her hands up both sides of his groin, over his abdomen back to his chest. She kneaded his nipples as she pushed her own more firmly against his back. Running her fingers back around his ribs she gripped his buttocks with her fingernails as she clamped onto his shoulder with her teeth.

Another shiver ran through him.

She raised her mouth back to his ear. "I told you not to be scared, Ryan. I'm not going to hurt you, I promise. I'm only interested in giving you pleasure, not pain, and I may come close to the line in pursuit of that mission, but I will not cross it, I assure you."

"I'm not shaking through fear anymore, Monica, just...anticipation," he assured her.

"Anticipation is good." She ran her chin down his neck. "It heightens our senses and kick-starts our adrenaline." She ran her hands down both sides of his ribs and pressed her fingernails into his hips, pulling him closer to her. "Do you feel your juices starting to flow, Ryan?"

"So much so I'm afraid the teenager in me is still going to embarrass himself before he gets to the finish line."

She pressed her lips against his spine as her hands came around him to cradle his balls. "If that were to happen I would take it as a compliment. I told you before, what turns me on, is turning you on. It pleases me to give you pleasure, Ryan; you need to understand that."

He let out a deep breath as he closed his eyes and dropped his head back towards her. "Then you should be the happiest girl from happy town right now because I am on cloud fucking nine."

She chuckled against his skin. "Not yet I'm not, but let's see what we can do about that, shall we?"

She moved around to face him again and gently pushed him back, so he sat on the edge of the bed.

Standing between his legs, she cradled his head positioning one of her breasts in front of his mouth. "Have your first taste, Ryan."

His eyes were glued to hers as he extended his tongue and tentatively circled her nipple. She threaded her fingers into his hair, pulling him closer, so he closed his eyes and took her fully into his mouth.

Releasing his head she grasped his shoulders and pushed him down to lay flat on the bed with his feet still remaining on the floor. She bent and picked up one foot, removed the shoe and sock then repeated the process with the other. This complete, she pulled at the bottom of his jeans taking them off completely.

She ran her fingernails up the back of his calves and around to run up the insides of his thighs. "Now, it's my turn to taste."

He took in a sharp breath as she ran her tongue down the length of his penis, then cried out as she took him in her mouth. He clung to the bedspread for dear life, terrified in case he touched her, and she stopped the glorious oral onslaught she was putting his body through.

"Monica," he cried out. "I'm sorry but if you continue doing that I'm not going to last much longer."

She released him, stood up and slowly started undoing her jeans. "I told you before, Ryan, you don't have to be sorry for that. It's taken me thirty years to get you into bed. We're not going anywhere until we get this right, and we have all the time we could possibly need."

She stepped out of the remainder of her clothing, so she too was completely naked.

Ryan lifted his head to look at her from head to foot. "You are absolutely blowing my mind."

She half smiled. "Well, I suppose your mind just as well be next on my list, but I'll get to all of you, eventually."

She reached into the bedside drawer and pulled out a condom. Holding it between her teeth, she crawled up the bed above him and then dropped it on his chest.

"I'd like you to put that on now, Ryan," she instructed.

He complied.

She hovered over him on all fours and ran a hand all the way down his chest, abdomen and ended on his cock, which she gently stroked a few times before taking him fully in her hand. She angled herself and started rubbing his tip against her clit, circling it, then running it down her folds to end back at her clit again, now covered in her own juices.

"My God, that feels amazing, Monica," he breathed.

"It's not too shabby from my side either; I assure you."

She took him into herself to the hilt and rubbed her pelvic bone against his, making him cry out again as he writhed beneath her.

She raised herself off his shaft and held it flat against him as she rubbed herself against him. She could feel they were both getting close so did a few more strokes and then took him inside her again, riding him vigorously as her fingernails dug into both of his breasts.

He cried out as he came so she clamped down hard on him, rubbing her clit forcefully against him while she could feel his penis pulsating inside her enabling her own orgasm to erupt.

Monica slid off Ryan and rested her head on her elbow beside him waiting for his lungs to replenish.

He turned his head to look at her. "I'm officially in awe of you now; you know that, right?"

She smiled. "Yep, I'm like the eighth wonder of the world."

"What now? I take it you're not big on cuddling?" he teased.

She raised one eyebrow. "And there was me thinking Americans didn't have a sense of humour."

"I'm only half American remember. I obviously get my quick wit from my father's side." He smiled.

She patted his cheek. "That must be a great comfort to you, Congressman. Now, why don't you have a little rest and bask in all your comical glory while I get some work done?"

"What makes you think I need a rest?"

"Don't you?"

He half shrugged. "You don't need a rest?"

She looked confused. "Why would I?"

He laughed. "Should I be insulted by that response?"

She smiled. "That would be a pointless waste of your time and a great waste of your energy, which I'm sure we can put to much better use later. I'm not finished with you yet, Ryan."

He rolled onto his side to face her. "I can't tell you how happy I am to hear you say that."

"Well, look who's suddenly grown a pair. What happened to the scared little teenager I had in front of me a short while ago?"

"He got laid and suddenly reached puberty. It was very liberating actually." He grinned.

She chuckled. "I'm glad I could, in my own small way, do my part to alleviate some of your less favourite childhood memories."

"There was nothing small about it; believe me." His expression turned serious, and he tentatively lifted his hand

and pushed some hair back from her face. "I'm in way over my head right now, and I can't believe how amazing it feels, and I can't seem to get enough of it."

She took hold of his hand and laid it on the bed between them but didn't release it. "Don't get confused about what we're doing here, Ryan. The last thing I want to do is hurt you, but I will if you let me, albeit unintentionally."

"I don't think you do anything unintentionally, but be that as it may, you need to stop worrying about me. I'm a big boy now, and it's about time I grew up, well beyond time really."

"Being a grown up can be overrated you know. Besides, it's not like you're pitching for a grown-up job or anything. Surely being Commander in Chief and the leader of the free world can't be that difficult," she teased.

"When you put it that way, it does sound like a walk in the park, don't you think?"

Chapter Eight

Ryan opened his eyes and was initially a little disorientated until his afternoon exploits came back to him and a smile split his face. Monica had warned him not to get confused, and whether he was or not, he had never felt more alive.

He got to his feet, putting on a robe he exited his bedroom looking for the source of his obsession. He found her at her desk in her own robe, tapping furiously at her laptop. He approached her slowly.

"For somebody that didn't need a rest, you did a superb impression of Rip Van Winkle." Her fingers didn't miss a beat.

He breathed out a laugh. "That's impressive. You seemed so engrossed in whatever it is you're doing I didn't realise you knew I was here."

"I'm incredibly good at multitasking."

"Is there anything you're not incredibly good at?"

She stopped typing and looked up at him as if seriously considering his question. "Dancing," she said honestly. "It completely eludes me. For some reason when I'm on the dance floor, I have the natural rhythm of a maggot."

He sat down in front of her with a smile. "I wouldn't worry too much about that, Monica. If it's any conciliation, there are other ways to get sweaty while rubbing up against someone, and in that, you excel."

She smiled smugly. "I do, don't I."

"Mind-blowingly so."

She sat back in her chair and looked him up and down like a lion that was about to pounce. Ryan could feel his pulse starting to race in anticipation of what was going through her mind.

He swallowed deeply. "What are you thinking about right now?"

"I'm thinking I have a lot of work to do."

He raised his eyebrows in surprise. "Oh? That's not where I thought you were going with the look that was on your face."

She smiled. "I haven't finished yet." She sat up in her chair and leant on her desk towards him. "So with that in mind, I'm thinking I'll have dinner brought up to us this evening. I'll make them bring candles and shit to keep the whole romantic facade going, but then after we've eaten, I'll be able to continue working. Is that acceptable to you?"

He nodded slowly. "As you wish."

She raised one side of her mouth. "So amenable, Congressman. You really should try to be more assertive sometimes, you know?"

Her comment for some reason annoyed him. "Be more like your brother, you mean?" he challenged.

Her face lost all expression. "Not where I was going, no."

"But that would make me more like your perfect man, wouldn't it? That's what you're looking for?" he taunted.

"I don't believe there is any such thing as the perfect man, certainly not for me anyway, and I'm not looking for anything. I thought I'd made that perfectly clear, Ryan."

He let out a deep breath. "You have. It doesn't mean I have to like it, though?"

She grinned. "Now, that's what I'm talking about. Say what you mean, tell people how you honestly feel, and that way you might end up with what you genuinely want."

He looked at her seriously. "Right now, all I want is to be back inside you. Is that what you mean?"

Her grin grew wider. "It's a start." She got up and walked around her desk, perching on the front of it beside him. "I've got an appointment in the morning with one of my personal trainers which I don't want to cancel, so I'm thinking that if you meet me in the gym, we can then go through to the spa and spend the day together. Do the whole joint massages, giggling in the hot tub thing. The usual crap people do when they're supposed to be madly in love or lust or whatever?"

"Fine," he said flatly.

"I know this is frustrating, Ryan, but we shouldn't have to wait much longer. We'll hear from Nicky soon, I'm sure, and then all of this role-playing madness will be behind us."

"And then you can go back to your normal life and forget all about me again because to you I am so easily controlled and dismissed. You have no idea of the man I am or the things I'm capable of," he said almost bitterly.

"There's too much history between us for me ever to forget you, Ryan, and we are making more with each passing second."

"But that's all we'll ever have though as far as your concerned isn't it, just history? There's not the slightest thought in your brain, not one part of you could ever believe that we could have a future?"

She smiled sadly. "I'm not sure where all of this is coming from, but let me tell you what I truly believe from the bottom of my soul and that's that I'm not the right woman for you, Ryan."

"What you mean is, I'm not the right man for you?"

She half shrugged. "Maybe I do, because there is no right man for me. I wouldn't allow it. I'm not just damaged, Ryan, I'm broken, remember, and there's nobody out there that's going to come along and be able to fix me."

He looked at her seriously. "I think you're wrong about that. I believe deep down you are looking for a man like your brother, or your father. I think that will be the only thing that will finally make you tick."

She stood. "Then you would be wrong. Do you remember what kind of man my father was? I know you were young but you were old enough to know a little of the way he earned a living."

"I've heard the stories the same as everybody else. What's your point?"

"My point is that my father ruled his empire with an iron fist and there are many people that are no longer around because of it, either by his own hand or by his order, which is irrelevant as the outcome was the same. To you and everybody else the things he did can remain just stories that you tell your children to make them behave, but to me, that's my heritage and I fight tooth and nail every day of my life to deny it. I am the spawn of the devil, Ryan, and you may forget that sometimes but I never can because if anything, I think my brother may be worse."

"Worse?" He drew his eyebrows together. "Monica, are you frightened of your brother?"

She gave a humourless chuckle. "Everybody should be frightened of my brother, Congressman, if they have any common sense, but that's a story for another time. Maybe. Now," she took hold of his hands and pulled him to his feet, "we both smell like horses and sex. Let's see what we can do about at least one of those, shall we?"

She led him through her own bedroom this time into her large bathroom and turned on the shower. The multiple water jets sprang to life.

She turned to him, pulling at the belt on his robe. "Let's not waste time wondering about the future, when we have a very appealing present to contend with."

She ran her hands up his chest and pushed the robe off his shoulders until it pooled on the floor around his feet.

She looked all the way down him then back to his eyes. "Very appealing indeed."

She went to step back away from him, but he grabbed the back of her neck holding her in place.

"Kiss me," he begged, "please. I know it's not something you usually do, I know it does nothing for you, but just this once, indulge me."

She looked at the overwhelming desperation in his eyes and momentarily softened. "I can hardly lecture you on standing up for yourself and asking for what you want, only to deny you when you do, now, can I? But I have a better idea. You kiss me."

He seemed to take a few seconds to register what she had just said. Very slowly he brought his face closer to hers, expecting any moment that she would pull away or stop him somehow. When she didn't, he tentatively placed his lips against hers for the slightest of pecks.

She smiled. "That's the sort of kiss you give your grandmother on her death bed. My gay friend kisses me more passionately. Surely when you have a naked trollop alone with you in the shower you can do better than that, Congressman?" she teased.

He smiled back and started to relax. "But you're not naked, yet."

Her hands dropped to her own belt, which she undid and threw the robe on the floor. "I am now, and if you want to do this thing, you have to do it properly, at least, so, show me what you've got, Ryan."

He pounced on her, cradling her head in the crook of his elbow as his tongue plundered her mouth. He pushed her up against the shower wall, planting them both under the huge metal plate above them, making them both feel like they were standing in warm rain while the side jets pummelled their naked bodies.

She gasped for air when he released her. "Wow, look who's actually got fire in their belly, Congressman. I hope you don't kiss babies like that when you're campaigning?"

He pressed his lips against her temple. "Ryan," he breathed.

"I'm sorry?"

"I want you to call me Ryan." His lips moved to her ear. "Not Congressman, that's my job. When I'm with you, I just want to be Ryan."

"You don't like people calling you, Congressman? I would have thought you would want it sung from the rooftops."

He threaded his fingers into her hair while his lips ran down her neck. "I have no issue when other people do it. When you do it, however, you have a knack for making it sound like ridicule." He smiled against her shoulder.

She chuckled. "That's because when I do it, Ryan, I'm usually taking the piss."

He pulled back to look at her. "I am well aware of that, and for the most part, it amuses me, but from now on, when we're alone and naked, I want you to call me Ryan."

"I could probably do that, but," she ran her hand down his chest, "for the most part, when we're alone and naked," she slowly stroked his penis making it stand to attention, "why don't we keep all conversation to a minimum?"

He closed his eyes and let out a deep breath. "Yeah, yours is a much better plan."

"I think so too," she agreed as she stepped away from him reached into the nearest drawer and pulled out a condom.

Taking hold of his penis again, she caressed it with one hand while attaching the condom with the other. Cradling his balls, she circled his nipple with her tongue. He took in a sharp breath as he stumbled back against the wall. She rubbed the tip of his cock against her clit arousing herself as well as him.

She turned around and pressed her back up against him. "You wanted to be back inside me, Ryan, so what are you waiting for?"

He put his mouth to her ear. "Permission."

She looked over her shoulder at him. "That's a schoolboy error, Ryan. It's always much more rewarding to ask for forgiveness once you've done just what you want, but if it's permission you need, then you have it."

She took hold of his hands and brought them around to cradle her breasts, massaging them deeply while rubbing his cock between her arse cheeks.

Ryan cried out his enjoyment. "You're actually letting me touch you?" he breathed.

"Technically, I'm touching myself, I'm just using your hands to do it, now stop talking and fuck me, Ryan."

He spun them both around, so she was facing the wall that she pressed her hands against while he dipped his knees to enable himself to slam inside her.

She took in a sharp breath then slightly chuckled. "Now, that's what I'm talking about. Give me your hands again."

He complied.

She rested one on the wall in front of them to give them both leverage to push up against and the other she ran down her body then covering his middle finger with her own she started caressing her clit.

He cried out again as his pounding intensified and she increased the tempo on her clit to follow suit.

"Monica," he screamed, "I'm going to come."

"Do it, I'm right there with you," she breathed before crying out her orgasm with Ryan immediately behind her.

He rested his head on her shoulder while his breathing returned to somewhat normal. "I've never known a woman quite like you before. How can you tell me you're broken when you make me feel like I've never been this complete in my whole life?"

"It's an illusion, Ryan, nothing more. You've taken a break from your life, from your reality, and who doesn't enjoy a good holiday, and this is a fantasy you were obviously long overdue for, but it's not real, so I will tell you again, don't get confused by it."

"What if I prefer this fantasy to my own reality? What if I decide I don't want to go back to my old life where everything is for appearances and nothing is just about me and what I want?"

"That could be a mistake, Ryan, if it had anything to do with me and, you'd end up getting your arse kicked." She turned to face him. "If you want to change your life then change it, but you're going to have to do it on your own and to suit yourself because I am nobody's saviour, I assure you."

He contemplated her words for a moment then smiled. "I'm not so sure about that, but I guess time will tell."

Chapter Nine

      Ryan entered the gym the following morning fully expecting to have to amuse himself for a while assuming she would be in one of the side rooms having a private lesson. He certainly did not expect to find her in the middle of the gymnasium on the training mat going blow for blow with a monster of a man twice her size. In her tight yoga pants and cropped sports bra top and with her hair braided down her back she could quite easily have passed for a teenager from a distance, but the aggression coming from her in wave after wave of high kicks, punches, and body blows was all the self-assured woman he was coming to know better with each passing day. He could hardly keep up with watching the pair of them they were moving so fast, but he couldn't seem to take his eyes from her. There was no other word to describe her; she was magnificent.

      When they finally finished pulverising each other, they bowed slightly then laughed as they high-fived, she picked up her towel from the floor and a bottle of water and came over to join him.

"Well, that was...impressive," he acknowledged. "I know you said you could look after yourself, but I was expecting to see...well, I don't know what I was expecting to see, to be honest, but it certainly wasn't that."

She half laughed as she gasped for air, guzzled some water and started dabbing her towel on her sweat covered chest. "I have warned you on a few occasions that I could kick your arse, Congressman. Now perhaps you will believe me?" she teased.

He slowly nodded with a smile. "I have been so advised and am totally on board with it. What type of fighting was that?"

"That was a mixture of all sorts I suppose. I've tried them all at some time or another but prefer just to pick and mix."

"How come you do it out in the open and don't have a private lesson somewhere. You don't think it unseemly for the proprietor of this establishment to be seen kicking the crap out of someone?" he teased.

"Not in the slightest. I like people to know that I'm dangerous, it tends to save time and make them slightly less inclined to piss me off."

He looked at her in awe. "I envy you that. It must be amazing to be that carefree all the time and just let loose."

She raised one side of her mouth. "You want to go a few rounds and find out, Congressman?"

"Err, no thank you. I don't have the benefit of the Secret Service with me right now so will give the ass-kicking a miss."

"Coward," she teased with a grin.

"You're right I am, and I freely admit it. I think fear gets a bad rap because there is nothing wrong with being intelligent enough to know when you're outmatched."

She smiled as she took another mouthful of her water. "I believe you're braver than you think you are. You've spent three days with me now, and I haven't made you cry once. That in itself is impressive."

He grinned. "I've come close a few times I can assure you."

"And yet somehow you managed to soldier on."

"When you put it that way I suppose it is impressive, yes."

"So is the brave little congressman ready for his pampering day now?"

"Indeed, I am."

Monica showered then they got massages together, took a swim then had lunch. Afterwards, she arranged for drinks to be taken to one of the more secluded outside hot tubs.

Ryan took a mouthful of his wine and then relaxed back into the warm bubbles. "Do you have days like this very often?"

"Not as often as I should. Every time I do, I always promise myself I'm going to do it more regularly but I just never seem to have the time because life stuff gets in the way."

"I think you have a perfect life, Monica," he said sincerely.

She half chuckled. "I can assure you I don't, Ryan, but thank you for saying that anyway."

"I mean it. You have a home that anybody would adore, you have a job that you love, and you do what you want when you want, with no one to please but yourself, and you don't have to take crap from anybody. What's not perfect about all of that?"

She raised her head to look at him with amusement all over her face. "Whose life are you talking about, because it certainly isn't mine?"

"How do you figure?"

"I'm constantly surrounded by millionaires or billionaires and in my experience, they aren't usually the easiest going bunch. They have high expectations and are not at all subtle when those expectations aren't met. Basically, taking crap from people is practically my job title."

He looked confused. "And yet, you're looking to extend your empire. I can't believe it's all about the money, so why do you do it?"

She slowly smiled. "Because you're right, I love it, and I can't imagine doing anything else."

He grinned back. "I knew it. Have you any idea how lucky you are? How rare that is?"

"I don't think it's that rare. I would say it was much more unusual for someone to dislike what they do as much as you do."

"I'm not sure dislike is the right word, I think I just find the whole thing...tedious may be more accurate." He ran wet hands through his hair pushing it back from his face. "I think the truth is I don't know how I feel about it most of the time, other than feeling that there must be something...more. There has to be a way that I can make things better, and if that means ruffling a few feathers to do it, I'm just going to have to find a way to do that without compromising myself or my career."

Monica drew her eyebrows together. "Seriously, Ryan, don't you ever wake up some mornings and think, fuck it?"

His face turned serious. "What would you say if I told you that I did, this morning in fact?"

"I would ask you why this morning, of all mornings."

"Maybe it's the magic of Eden; maybe it's the magnificent food or the superior wine cellar, or...maybe...it's you?"

"I'd stick with the food and wine if I were you, they would be much more reliable."

"I don't want to have to give you up, Monica. Can you honestly say you feel nothing for me, and that all of this is just one-sided because I don't think I believe that?"

"I don't belong in your world, Congressman, certainly not after all of our sordid past comes to light. Surely you see that?"

"You didn't answer my question."

"Neither did you," she challenged.

He let out a deep breath. "Okay, fine. Do I think you belong in my world; not for a New York minute, but not because of anything to do with your past, or your families past, but because you are too real to be able to stomach the Neverland that I live and breathe in. But then, I guess my counter-question to you, would be, what if that wasn't my world anymore? What if I just...?" He smiled. "What if I just bought a different ticket and changed trains? Now you have two questions to answer, so it's your turn."

She giggled. "Change trains? What genius put that pearl of wisdom in your brain?"

"Some trollop I met naked in a shower." He grinned. "Now, stop stalling and answer my questions."

"I don't know what you want me to say. I have told you before that none of this is real, but you're just not hearing me."

"Try me one more time," he encouraged.

"Do you think the last three days have been normal for me? I have a job to do, Ryan, a very demanding job actually. I don't spend my time riding horses, having picnics, afternoon sex sessions, and spa days. The reason you found me at the pool at two in the morning was that I had just finished work and like to swim before I sleep for a few short hours, and then I start my day all over again. You may live and breathe in Neverland, but I live and breathe something that closely resembles a workhouse, albeit a very luxurious one. You chose a path where you live your life in the spotlight and are destined for greatness; mine is very much lived in the shadows. And now you are saying what, that you're prepared to give all that up based on three days of knowing me? You are asking me to be the Wallace Simpson to your Prince Edward, and I am categorically telling you that you have the wrong girl."

"So what are you saying, that you need to change trains too?"

She threw her hands up in the air. "Oh, for the love of God, Ryan, will you please stop talking about trains. What I'm saying is I won't be changing anything, because I don't want to. Everything in my life is exactly where I want it to be, and as far as you not wanting to give me up, Ryan, I'm not yours to begin with, so giving me up, simply isn't your call."

He didn't look perturbed in the least. "You haven't answered my other question yet. Tell me you don't care about me?"

She smiled in spite of herself. "You're so like a dog with a bone, Congressman; you know that?"

He smiled back at her. "That's not an answer."

She opened her mouth to respond but hesitated and tilted her head.

"Well?" he prompted.

"Shh." She held up her hand to silence him and leant a little further to one side. "I think somebody's coming," she whispered.

He laughed. "Are you lying right now, so you don't have to answer the question?"

She smiled. "I'm not, I swear, so just shut up for a moment and follow my lead, okay?"

"Whatever you say, Mrs Simpson."

She giggled as she straddled his lap and took his head in her hands. "I said shut up, you delusional moron."

She pulled his head into her chest while continuing to giggle and pretending to whisper sweet nothings into his ear.

"Am I interrupting something?"

Monica looked up and saw Vincent standing there. "Vinnie." She went to get off of Ryan's lap but then stopped herself. "Are you alone?"

He nodded. "I am, so stop pretending to shag your fake boyfriend and introduce me to him, will you?"

"Of course, I will, darling."

She stood up and kissed Vincent on the lips then perched on the side of the hot tub and turned back to a very confused looking Ryan.

"Ryan Whittaker, let me introduce you to Vincent Marlon, one of my very best friends, and for his sins, Nicky's right-hand man. Vinnie, let me introduce you to Ryan, who is either going to be the President of the United States if Nicky's believes our bullshit and decides to play ball, or my next head gardener if he doesn't, the jury's still out on that one."

Vincent put his hand out, but Ryan looked completely flabbergasted.

Monica laughed. "It's fine, Ryan, Vinnie knows the whole story so you can completely relax."

"Yeah, it's okay mate, Moani Moani and me don't have any secrets, it's all good."

Ryan took his hand. "I'm sorry, I knew you two were close, of course, I just didn't know you were aware of our...situation."

"Talking of which," Monica interrupted, "what news is there from the lion's den? Is he going to play ball, or what?"

Vincent shrugged. "You know the deal with Nick and me when it comes to you, Moani. Your brother would quite literally trust me with his life because he knows, undoubtedly, that I would give mine to protect him without a second's hesitation, but when it comes to his baby sister, he knows how much I love you so plays his cards very close to his chest so as not put me in a position of split loyalties. I repay that respect by never asking him any questions."

She let out a deep breath. "So, you know nothing?"

"I wouldn't say nothing. He sent me here to tell you that he's coming here for dinner tonight to talk to you two and that he's bringing a date."

She drew her eyebrows together. "A date? Who?"

"He didn't say, and I didn't ask. He has also asked me to come along as well, so he's obviously in the mood for an audience."

"Something's not right. He loves nothing more than to make me squirm; he always has for what he considers my attitude flaws, but he usually does it in private. He knows I never take his shit lying down so he wouldn't trust me not to shout my mouth off and return his jibes in kind, so if he's bringing someone with him, she's not for audience purposes, she's a prop, and it has to have something to do with you." She looked at Ryan. "You don't think that it's Meredith, do you?"

Ryan's eyebrow shot up. "Meredith? Absolutely no way, how could it possibly be?"

"You're sure? Do you know where she is right now?"

"Of course, I do, she's in The Hamptons with her family."

"When was the last time you had any contact with her?" she persisted.

"A few days ago, but she knows nothing of any of this, I assure you."

"All due respect to your assurances, Ryan, but I would feel happier about it if you called her, just to make sure. If it is her, then we need to be prepared for it. I wouldn't call Meredith turning up a showstopper exactly, but the quicker you can start with the damage control the better."

He hesitated for only a moment then got to his feet. "Yeah, okay, I guess forewarned is forearmed." He got out and wrapped a towel around his waist then extended his hand to Vincent again. "It was good to meet you, Vincent, albeit under very unusual circumstances."

"Yeah, you too mate, and I'll see you tonight for whatever fun our evening has in store."

"Yes, I'm sure we'll all be awaiting that with baited breath." He turned to Monica. "I'll see you upstairs?"

She nodded. "I'll be up shortly."

He smiled and walked away.

Vincent watched him leave before turning back to Monica. "So, you're fucking him for real now?"

She shrugged. "That's not exactly the shock of the century, is it? You know I have the morals of an alley cat."

He half laughed. "I wouldn't be too hard on yourself, Moani Moani; he is very fuckable."

"Isn't he, though? I just couldn't seem to resist, for all of the thirty seconds that I tried that is." She smiled.

He grinned. "You always were big on willpower. So is this going to complicate matters now if this thing goes tits up with Nick?"

"What do you mean?"

"Are you going to get all emotional and shit if things don't go your way now that you have a genuine vested interest in him?"

She drew her eyebrows together. "When have you ever known me to get emotional and shit over anything?"

"I've never known you to piss this close to your doorstep before either, but that seems to be exactly what you've done."

She half shrugged. "Maybe you're right, and it wasn't the smartest move I've ever made, but we both know Nicky is going to do whatever he wants to, and all the tantrums in the world from me won't make a blind bit of difference."

"Then I guess we'll see what we see."

"Indeed, we will. Tell Nicky that I'll be serving dinner at my place and not in the main house. Let's try and keep the floorshow spectators to a minimum."

"I'll tell him."

He kissed her on the lips and walked away.

By the time Monica returned to her apartment, Ryan was sitting on the sofa with a drink in his hand.

"Did you manage to get hold of her?"

"I did," he confirmed as he got to his feet and came and stood in front of her. "She was just getting ready to go shopping with her mother. Whoever your brother is bringing with him, it isn't Meredith."

Monica half shrugged and let out a deep breath. "Then I guess we will just have to wait and see, won't we? I suppose I'd better go and get ready for our fun packed evening."

"Monica wait, I need to ask you something. Why did your mind automatically go to Meredith? Does the fact of her bother you?"

She drew her eyebrows together. "What do you mean?"

"Well, does it…does she…does the fact of her being in my life make you feel like the other woman in all of this?"

She grinned. "Technically, I am the other woman, Ryan, to all intents and purposes."

"But ours, Meredith and I, it isn't a meeting of two hearts, it's far more practical than that. You do understand that, don't you?"

"So, not the romance of the century then, is that what you're saying?" she teased.

He shook his head. "Not remotely, and I would hate for you to think otherwise and feel you were doing anything wrong."

She put a hand on his cheek. "You are very sweet sometimes, Congressman, you know that," she lightly tapped his face, "perhaps a little too sweet? The fact that it would even enter your mind that Meredith would bother me, or doing something wrong would, for that matter, shows just how poles apart the two of us truly are." She kissed his other cheek.

"So, it doesn't bother you?"

"Very little in this life bothers me, Ryan, but we're about to have dinner with one of the few exceptions to that rule, so if you'll excuse me, I need to go and put my game face on." She turned to walk away.

"Is that all it takes to protect yourself from your brother? The right outfit and a perfect face of make-up? If that's the case what do you think I should wear? Is he a leg man or a boob man?" he teased.

Monica turned back to face him with a serious expression on her face. "Please don't be flippant with Nicky this evening, Ryan. You have no idea how dangerous it is just being in his company."

He still looked slightly amused. "When are you going to realise that I am a grown man now, who has made more that his fair share of hard decisions in my time. I wouldn't be in the position I am now if I hadn't. I'll admit that I do have a special kind of weakness towards my mother because I feel that I owe her a lot so tend to accommodate her whenever possible, but please do not underestimate me, Monica, because I do know how to play hardball."

She took hold of his hand and led him to the sofa to sit beside him. "In the interests of you having some understanding of what sort of man you will be facing this evening, I am going to tell you something that I have never told a living soul. I'm only going to say this once and then we are never going to speak of it again. Agreed?"

He nodded. "Go on?"

She took a deep breath. "The reoccurring nightmare that I have, I think you're right and it's probably a memory that my subconscious is trying to remind me of but I don't think I want to know. It's always jumbled and doesn't make any sense, but I see blood, a lot of blood, I hear my mother's voice calling out to me, and then I see Nicky. He's younger, of course, but he has hold of me and I'm frightened. From everything I've been told of that night, I found my mother dead in the swimming pool, so why do I keep hearing her voice?"

Ryan looked confused. "I don't understand what you're trying to say to me, Monica?"

"What if..." she licked her dry lips, "what if my mother wasn't dead? What if Nicky was trying to hurt me and my mother caught him?"

He raised his eyebrows in shock. "You think he was trying to hurt you and your mother interrupted him so he killed her?"

"I'm not sure but I'd be lying if I said it hadn't crossed my mind. With all the evidence pointing to my father's guilt, not once has my brother acknowledged it, nor did he turn his back on him for killing his mother. Why would he do that unless he knew for a fact that my father was innocent?"

Ryan looked shell-shocked. "Do you recall him trying to hurt you again, since that night?"

"There was no need after that night because whatever threat he felt I posed to him became irrelevant. He likes to tell me how I was the apple of my father's eye, but with my father out of the equation, that didn't matter anymore."

"You really think he would be capable of doing that?"

"I honestly don't know, Ryan, but what I do know is that Nicky doesn't tolerate competition, he eliminates it. You'll do well to remember that."

Ryan slowly nodded. "I've been so advised," he acknowledged quietly.

Chapter Ten

When Monica opened the door to her apartment the first thing that struck her was why it was only Nicky and Vinnie standing there.

Nick smiled warmly. "Ecca. So lovely of you to invite us all over like this." He kissed the top of her head as he walked passed her.

She raised her eyebrows to Vincent in an unasked question as to where the third party was and he only shrugged in response.

Nick walked into the living room and outwardly greeted his childhood friend warmly. "Ryan, it's been a long time. How have you been?" He shook his hand briefly before walking over to the bar to fix himself a drink.

"I've been well, thank you, Nick, and you?"

"Good, yes, very good in point of fact." He took a mouthful of his drink. "So, you're doing my sister, I understand. That must be...entertaining. From what I hear, she's quite a provocative woman."

"Seriously, Nicky," Monica interrupted. "We're not in deliverance country now. Can't you a least try to be civilised?"

He looked amused. "Don't be so sensitive little sister. I'm actually congratulating you. It might have taken you a few years, but you bagged him in the end, or I suppose bedded him would be more accurate."

She rolled her eyes while trying not to rise to the bait. "Talking of which, I thought you were bringing a date with you? Where is she?"

"All in good time, Ecca. She'll be along shortly. I've left word at the front desk for them to bring her on up when she arrives."

"Anyone I know?" Monica tried to make her voice sound casual and uncaring but to no avail.

It didn't fool her brother for a second and he smirked. "I said, all in good time, Ecca." He turned his attention back to Ryan. "So, my old friend, it appears that my sister's sex life is off limits and not open to debate, so why don't you let me know what else you've been up to? The White House is in your sights, I hear? Well, that's impressive, tell me about it?"

Monica sat and listened to her brother make small talk, seemingly the most pleasant, easy going man in the world. She could almost see the wheels turning in Nick's head with every word that came out of Ryan's mouth. She could tell it was all he could do not to pounce and unleash whatever it was he had up his sleeve.

After about twenty minutes she felt fit to explode at all the platitudes she'd heard when there was a knock on the door.

She went to get up but Nick stopped her.

"Allow me, Ecca; you stay where you are. It's the least I can do considering how you've been slaving over our dinner all afternoon." He smiled. "Well, I'm sure the phone call you made to the kitchen was rather exhausting. All that decision making needed for what wine to put with which course must have been positively draining?"

She smiled tightly. "It must have been, Nicky, because I've never felt more sick and tired in my life."

"Ah," he mock sympathised, "perhaps you're coming down with something? Give it a moment or two and I'm sure you're going to rally. Back in a jiff." He smiled again as he went to answer the door.

Monica thought momentarily that she must be hallucinating when he returned with Annabel Whittaker on his arm.

Ryan jumped to his feet. "Mother? What on earth are you doing here? I thought I made myself clear when I told you to go home."

"Good evening, Ryan. Didn't I tell you to leave everything to me? Surely you didn't think for one moment that I would just scurry off with my tail between my legs and leave you defenceless just to fend for yourself?" She glanced momentarily in Monica's direction. "I'm made of sterner stuff than that, Ryan, as all in this room would do well to remember."

Nick put his arm around Annabel's shoulder. "How heart-warming. Do you hear how much your Mummy loves you, Ryan? Almost enough to bring a tear to my eye."

Ryan was speechless.

Nick turned his attention to Monica. "Nothing to say, Ecca?"

She looked at her brother flatly. "You have got to be shitting me? How the fuck did you two cross paths again?"

He wagged his finger at her. "Nah, uh, uh, little sister. Wasn't it you that lectured me earlier on being civilised? Annabel is a guest in your home, Ecca, and she should be welcomed properly, don't you think? Please tell me you are going to play nice?"

Monica glared at Annabel before focusing all of her venom back on her brother. "What I think is, I am not in the habit of welcoming anyone, be it properly or otherwise, back into my home once I have thrown them out, and I don't want her here, so I strongly suggest she leaves, right now."

Nick grinned. "Yeah, well, I don't want to be this charming and good looking but some crosses we just have to bear, little sister. Being that you want something from me, and need me to stay right now, let's just say for argument's sake that Annabel is *my* guest this evening then. That being said, I strongly suggest that you get over yourself, put your claws away, and *play nice*. Agreed?"

Monica shook her head, slowly closed her eyes, and let out a deep breath. "Fine, you win. Just get on with it, Nicky, so we can get this farce over and done with."

Nick clapped his hands together. "That's the spirit, and you're right, of course, we really should get on with it. Annabel, why don't you take a seat and I'll get you a drink."

As Annabel walked passed Monica, she looked down at her smugly. "I told you this wasn't over. Perhaps, this time, you'll remember your place and realise just how unimportant your role is in all of this?"

Monica kept her eyes directly on Annabel's. "Nicky, can you please tell your guest that if she opens her mouth again to me in that condescending manner, I'm going to be very tempted to put my fist in it."

"Well, so much for playing nicely," Nick said under his breath. "Annabel, be a dear, would you, and just take your seat. Also, for all our sakes, knowing my sister as I do, let me assure you that for you to assume she is joking right now, or won't make good on her word, would be a grave error of judgement, so it would be great if you could just button it, okay?"

Monica could see Annabel swallow her retort as she flounced over to take her seat on one of the other sofas without comment.

"Right then, that's better." Nick handed Annabel a drink with a smile. "So, we should perhaps start at the beginning, I suppose, which will tie in quite nicely with the question you asked a moment ago, Ecca, when Annabel first arrived and that was... how did we meet again after all these years?"

He leisurely poured himself another drink, knowing all eyes were on him and waiting for his next words but he waited until he casually took his seat, leant back and crossed his legs.

"Annabel came to see me today, and was quite anxious to clear up any misunderstandings there may be as to what my answers would be should certain questions be asked of me in the very near future. We hashed it out for a little while, as far be it for me to be difficult, and, as I'm sure everybody in this room will be happy to hear, we finally came to an understanding, didn't we, dear?" He patted Annabel's knee affectionately.

"Indeed, we did, Nicholas," she proclaimed as though she were some sort of conquering hero.

Ryan sat forward in his chair. "What sort of understanding? Mother, would you please tell me exactly what is going on here?"

"For crying out loud, Nicky," Monica interrupted. "Will you please cut the crap, stop picking and choosing your words, and start calling a spade a fucking spade. I may know how you operate, but Ryan doesn't, so before we all lose the will to live, will you just, for the love of God, speak plainly?"

Nick drained his glass and got to his feet. "You're turning into quite the little buzzkill lately, Ecca, do you know that?" he teased.

Monica sat up in her chair. "Nicky!" she warned.

He held up his hands to silence her. "Okay, fine." He took a deep breath as he poured himself another drink.

"Sorry, Ryan, I seem to be the only one in my family with a flair for the dramatic, or any sort of finesse for that matter, so this is the situation. Your mother, understandably so, would much rather specific pictures and films that I have in my possession didn't see the light of day. To add to which, she also requires that I have a selective memory when your background people come sniffing around and asking me questions. Fortunately for you, I am so inclined to scratch your back as it were, providing of course, that you are prepared to scratch mine." He turned towards Monica. "Plain enough for you, little sister, or do I need to be more specific?"

"What exactly do you mean by me scratching your back, Nick? What will that involve?" Ryan intervened.

Nick half laughed. "Clearly I do. To put it bluntly, Ryan, scratching my back will involve anything I say it does. Whatever I need, if it's within your remit, you will deliver." He smiled. "Any more questions?"

"I have one," Monica interrupted. "Where exactly did this meeting between you and Ryan's mother take place?"

Nick tried to keep the amusement out of his facial expression. "Annabel was kind enough to come and see me at my office earlier today. Why?" he asked smugly.

Monica slammed her drink down on a side table while turning towards Annabel. "You stupid bitch," she fumed.

"I beg your pardon," Annabel said indignantly.

"You don't have the first fucking idea of what you've done, do you?" Monica challenged.

Annabel stuck her chin out. "I did what needed to be done, so why don't you just be quiet and let the grown-ups talk, there's a good girl."

"And there it is," Monica yelled as she jumped to her feet.

"Grab her, Vince, for fucks sake!" Nick shouted.

For a man Vincent's size, he was on his feet in a split second and grabbed Monica, seemingly out of mid-air, on a trajectory directly heading for Annabel Whittaker.

"Calm down, Moani Moani, please," Vincent pleaded. "This is exactly the emotional shit I was worried about. You know I can't let you at her. It's obviously why Nick brought me here in the first place. I love you, babe, but I also have a job to do so you've got to let me do it."

Annabel leant back in her chair and put a hand to her chest. "My God, she's an animal," she screeched.

"Two things, dear, sweet, Annabel," Nick said as he put a hand on her shoulder. "Firstly, I did warn you not to take her words of warning lightly, so that little outburst was entirely your doing. And secondly, if you ever say anything derogatory about my sister again within my earshot, if you even think it in my presence, I'm going to show you exactly who the real animal in this family is. Do we understand each other, Annabel?"

Annabel swallowed the lump of fear that had formed in her throat by the look of pure murder in Nick's eyes and she slowly nodded.

He squeezed her shoulder tighter. "I need you to use your words, dear. Tell me that you completely understand the rules when it comes to my sister, and make me believe you."

Annabel whined in spite of herself. "I understand, Nicholas, completely, and I'm sorry if I caused any offence. It was not intentional." There was an imploring tone to her voice, practically begging for his forgiveness.

He smiled at her as he released his grip and gave her shoulder a few gentle taps. "That's better."

Monica closed her eyes as she took several deep breaths into her lungs, trying desperately to regain her composure.

"Are you okay now?" Vincent asked her quietly.

She nodded. "I'm okay."

He slowly released her and she retook her seat.

Nick started chuckling having regained his sense of humour. "Well, this evening is even more entertaining than I thought it was going to be. Maybe we should do it more often, Ecca, what do you think? Maybe make it an annual thing or something?" he taunted.

Monica ignored him and refocused on Annabel. "You have systematically taken a bad situation, and made it a thousand times worse."

Annabel licked her dry lips and spared a glance in Nick's direction before replying to Monica. "Concessions were necessary, of course, but that doesn't change the outcome, the whole point of this, which is nothing will now stand in the way of my son's future plans. Wasn't that exactly what you, yourself were trying to secure?"

Monica slowly shook her head in disbelief. "He would have recorded your whole visit, your entire conversation, you brainless bint."

Annabel hesitantly looked at Nick. "You did?"

Nick raised his eyebrows. "Did I forget to mention that? Oops - my bad. It must have completely slipped my mind."

Annabel cleared her throat and turned back to Monica. "Well, it changes nothing. We've reached an agreement and that's all that matters."

Monica threw her hands in the air. "It changes everything, you moron. Can you be this dense?"

Annabel pursed her lips tightly in objection to the way she was being spoken to. "Why don't you explain it to me then?"

Monica took another deep breath, drawing of every bit on self-control she possessed. "The previous situation, while tricky, could have if necessary been overcome. Not only did everything my brother had on you happen practically a lifetime ago, Ryan could have simply claimed the sins of the father loophole, or the sins of the mother, as the case may be, and perhaps the worst that could happen would be you would have had to step back from the public eye in connection with his campaign. Now," she glared at Nick and fumed anew at the self-satisfied look on his face. She took another deep breath. "Now, he has you on tape, in the present day, bribing him to keep quiet by making a deal. That's defrauding the public. I have no doubt in my mind that you also made assurances on Ryan's behalf as well, assuring Nick of Ryan's cooperation and involving another person. That's a conspiracy."

Nick started chuckling again. "Yeah, you're right, Ecca, that's exactly what she did. She was absolutely perfect, bless her, it was as though I'd given her a script."

Ryan sat forward and buried his face in his hands. "Oh, Mother. What have you done?" he breathed.

"Well, I...I...I thought..."

"The only way now," Monica interrupted her, "for Ryan to have any chance of getting out of my brother's clutches and be his own man, is to renounce you publically, deny all knowledge of your plans, strongly recommend that charges be brought against you, and you would have to be prosecuted to the fullest extent of the law."

Nick started clapping. "Yep, right again, little sister." He nudged Annabel with his elbow. "She is so smart, don't you think, it makes me proud."

Annabel looked like she was going vomit or cry or perhaps even both at the same time.

"Oh, relax, Annabel," Nick continued putting a hand on her back in a reassuring manner, "there's no need to fret. Your son has no intention of doing that to you, do you, Ryan?"

Ryan looked up at his mother for a moment and then turned to Nick. "No, no I don't."

"Think very carefully before you say any more, Ryan, please," Monica warned. "The next words out of your mouth could impact your entire future and you need to understand that."

He looked at her. "What is there to think about, Monica? Do you seriously expect me to have my own mother arrested and perhaps even send her to prison? Do you actually think that's an option for me?"

She smiled sadly. "Then I'm sorry. My worst fears have been realised, and Nicky owns you now. I wanted more than anything to spare you that fate; I really did, you deserved better."

He had a look of total devastation. "I thank you for trying, and no matter what happens, I will always be grateful."

"Ryan, I..." Annabel was struggling for words. "I'm sorry, my son, I didn't mean for any of this to happen and I only had your best interests at heart, but...but maybe it won't be so bad. I mean, this is after all how alliances are formed, and a man in Nicholas's position could prove very useful."

Monica got to her feet and Vincent was up and standing in front of her within the blink of an eye.

"Relax, Vinnie, I'm done. I just can't listen to anymore of this shit. I'm leaving." She looked at her brother. "Thank you, Nicky, for denying me the only favour I've ever asked of you. I'm truly feeling the love, big brother, and can't believe I ever doubted it."

Nick took hold of her wrist. "Oh, don't be like that, Ecca, there's no need to be upset. This was just too good a business opportunity to walk away from, that's all. It was practically the deal of a lifetime. But hey, it all worked out in the end. I'll keep my side of the bargain, your boy toy will get what he needs, so everyone's a winner, wouldn't you say?"

She looked at him flatly. "No, Nicky, not everyone wins, in fact, nobody does, just you, like always."

She walked passed him, grabbed a shawl from the coat rack and left her apartment without another word.

Chapter Eleven

Monica sat on the stone bench in the clock tower with her shawl around her shoulders and tried desperately to block out all of the evening's events. She lost track of how long she had been sitting there, being so overwhelmed by her complete failure in protecting Ryan from her brother.

Hearing footsteps in the doorway, she looked up to see Ryan standing there. She turned her head away from him without speaking and continued to stare out of the glassless window.

"I thought I might find you here," he said quietly.

"Congratulations. At least something has gone your way this evening," she said flatly.

He took another step closer to her. "It wasn't much of a leap, to be honest. You said you came here whenever people pissed you off so you could regain your inner calm or whatever, and after the evening we just had, well, I can only guess at the mood you are in right now, so it didn't exactly take a genius."

She huffed. "Just as well really. We seem to be a little short on the ground for genius thinking this evening."

"Neither of us could have foreseen what happened this evening, Monica, what my mother, of all people, instigated. There's no way we could have seen that coming."

She spun her head towards him. "Couldn't we? You think so? I know how my brother's mind works; I've lived with it for thirty-five years. I should have known that he would think you far too valuable an asset to walk away from and would find another way to get to you, if not through me, then some other way. You were right when you said my mind went straight to Meredith, and that was stupid of me. The connection between the two of you isn't nearly strong enough to warrant Nicky's attention. He would have known from the start that it was a marriage of convenience, as I did, and that you wouldn't give up everything for her if it stopped being quite so convenient. He knew your mother wouldn't let you, even if you wanted to." She let out a deep breath. "I should have realised that too, and I am so angry with myself that it didn't occur to me."

He came and sat beside her. "It's not down to you to think of everything, every eventuality. It's not your fault, none of this is. You should cut yourself some slack."

"Cutting myself some slack is the last thing in the world I should do. I wasted your time; I asked you to put your trust in me, which you did, and I...I let you down. I'm so sorry, Ryan."

He studied her beautiful face and saw all the emotions running across it. "I'm very tempted to risk getting my ass handed to me right now by putting my arm around you."

She raised one side of her mouth. "Still waiting for permission I see, Congressman? I told you before that that's a schoolboy error, have I taught you nothing?"

He smiled. "I'm not exactly waiting for permission, more trying to build my courage to ask for forgiveness if it all goes wrong."

She grinned. "Well, that's an improvement, I suppose." Her face straightened. "I think you've had your arse handed to you enough for one night, don't you? Besides, for once in my life I think a hug might actually be quite nice. Why don't we give it a try so I can see what all the fuss is about?"

He put his arm around her, pulling her closer to him and she rested her head against his shoulder. They sat there in silence for a few moments before Ryan spoke again.

"I think a big part of why you are being so hard on yourself is because you think your brother got one over on you, and that pisses you off way more than all of this other crap."

She remained silent.

Ryan gave her a little squeeze. "Come on, admit it. You can be honest with me. I promise I won't judge you in your little sibling rivalry."

Monica let out a deep breath. "Okay, fine. So it pisses me off when Nicky's smarter than I am. Why wouldn't it, it doesn't happen very often." She raised one side of her mouth.

He grinned. "That's more like it. I wouldn't exactly say it's the beaming smile that I'm looking for, but it's a step in the right direction, and right now I'll take what I can get."

"Why are you being so nice to me now? You should be so angry with me, furious, actually, that everything we have done, everything I put you through, has all been for nothing, and yet here you are, giving me comfort, and trying to cheer me up. Why?"

He rested his head on top of hers. "Isn't it obvious? It's because I've fallen in love with you, Monica, surely you know that?"

She tensed in his arms. "Ryan, please don't."

"There's no need to worry. I know you don't feel the same way about me right now, and you don't need to give me the 'don't get confused' speech again, because I'm not confused, in fact, quite the opposite, actually, I've never been more clear in my life. For the first time, ever, I know exactly how I feel, and I'm just sharing that with you, that's all."

"You don't know me, Ryan, not really. You may have known the child I was, but you've only known the adult I've become for a few days, which isn't nearly long enough for you to make that kind of statement."

"I know your heart."

"That's the last thing in the world that you know. How could you possibly, when I don't?"

"For some reason that's beyond me, you tend to spend so much of your time judging yourself, and finding yourself wanting. I don't agree because I look with better eyes than that."

"Perhaps you just need to remove the rose-coloured glasses from that superior vision of yours?"

"Why would I want to do that for a second, when I like the view perfectly well, just as it is?"

She slowly shook her head and closed her eyes. "Do you know what, Ryan, I don't have the energy to argue with you anymore over this. I know that it will all prove irrelevant anyway, as I'm sure when the Atlantic is between us again, then saner thoughts will prevail."

There was a heavy silence between them, and Monica could feel he had more to say but was certain that she didn't want to hear it.

She straightened in his arms. "I should stick with my first instincts. Cuddling out your problems is completely pointless, and it's giving me a stiff neck, so I'm done, thank you."

He reluctantly released her. "I want to be here for you and make you feel better, but I just don't know how to do that, I'm sorry."

The sad look in his eyes along with the desperation in his voice had Monica wanting to give him something, some sort of gesture, to make him feel as though he was assisting her in what he obviously considered to be her hour of need.

"Well," she half smiled. "If you want to make me feel better, how are you at foot massages?"

He smiled back. "You're actually in luck this evening, young lady, because if foot rubs were an Olympic event, I would be a gold medallist, even if I do so say myself."

"Is that right?" She pulled away from him to turn sideways and leant against the wall. "In that case," she slipped her shoes off and raised her legs, putting her feet on his lap. "Show me what you've got, Congressman. On your marks, get set, and go."

He set to his task and soon had her moaning out her appreciation at his skilled hands. Monica didn't want to spoil the more relaxed mood that had developed between them, but there were things she needed to know and things that needed to be said, ensuring Ryan knew precisely what the situation was now because of her failure.

She leant her head back and closed her eyes, preferring not to see his face turn sad again. "So what was the situation downstairs when you came looking for me? Have they all left yet?"

"No." He didn't stop his thumbs massaging her instep. "My mother and your brother are still busy putting their heads together, planning my future, but strangely enough, I seemed surplus to requirements."

"I'd get used to that if I were you. I meant what I said earlier, Ryan. Nicky owns you now. You are completely at his beck and call. I know the thought of your future didn't exactly have you emotionally rolling in puppies, and I hate to be the one to tell you this, but it just got a whole hell of a lot worse."

"I don't think so," he said dismissively, as though he didn't have a care in the world.

"Then you're mistaken. Nicky is not going to have an ace like you up his sleeve and not play you every chance he gets. The only possible way out would be for you to have something equally as damaging over him, and although I'm sure there would be plenty of dirt to choose from in his sordid little life, the only person that would have those types of details would be Vinnie, and he would die before he betrayed my brother. He's annoyingly loyal and not nearly as stupid as your mother to let something slip inadvertently."

"It doesn't matter. I have no interest in blackmailing my blackmailer, so the seedier aspects of Nick's life are irrelevant to me."

"You sound so resigned. I can't believe how well you're taking this. I'd be kicking and screaming all the way."

"There's nothing to kick and scream about because whatever Nick thinks he has in store for me isn't going to happen. I'm not going to do it." He bent and kissed the tip of her big toe.

She raised her head to look at him. "You make it sound like you have a choice, Ryan, and you don't. Refusing my brother is not an option for you. Please don't think that Nicky's bluffing, because, believe me, when push comes to shove, he won't back down. He'll destroy you in the blink of an eye if you don't play ball and not think twice about it."

He smiled. "I don't doubt it for a second, but I won't have to play ball if I don't pick up the bat."

She drew her eyebrows together. "What are you talking about, Ryan, you're not making any sense?"

He smiled. "I think I'm making perfect sense, but I'm not sure you want to hear it."

"Try me," she pushed.

He gave her feet one final squeeze then his hands stilled, and he just held onto them. "I'm not going to be jumping through any of your brother's hoops because I'm not going to run for president. I'm going to step down from office, withdraw from politics and live my own life for once. In short," he smiled, "I'm changing my ticket."

Her face lost all emotion. "Tell me why, Ryan, and be very specific."

"You don't have to worry, Monica, you aren't the reason, although I would be lying if I said you weren't the catalyst."

"That doesn't work for me, Ryan, and I don't want that sort of responsibility. You're just changing one Katlyn controller for another, don't you see? You must do what you want to do without any outside interference."

"But that's what I'm saying to you, this is what I want, but up until now I've been too stupid or too browbeaten or just too afraid to see it. I'm not going to let any of that stand in my way anymore. From this moment on I'm going to live my life exactly as I want to live it, and more importantly," he hesitated as he took a deep breath, "*where* I want to live it."

Monica still didn't look pleased. "Meaning?"

"Meaning, I'm going to move back to England. I'm finally ready to come home."

She let out the breath that she had been holding. "That's just what I'm afraid of. Do you seriously expect me to believe that you are going to uproot your life and move back here of all places, and I'm not the reason? You're getting wrapped up in the fantasy again, and you need to stop before you do something you are going to regret."

"Regrets have been my speciality up until now, Monica, but not this time. This time, my actions are all about me."

"I don't believe you, Ryan. Look me in the eye and tell me you're not thinking in the back of your mind that we have a future together?"

"Well," he half shrugged, "I guess that would be up to you. For my part, yes, I want you in my life, and I'm sure that given time, I could be the man you want me to be, the man you need me to be."

She shook her head in disbelief. "Why on earth would you want to be? According to you what I'm looking for is a mirror image of my brother. A soulless monster with a total disregard for anybody else's feelings. Why would you want to do that to yourself, even if you could?"

He slowly smiled. "I told you, I've fallen in love with you, but it's not only that. I feel like you have given me my life back, and I can finally breathe again, and I owe you for that. There is nothing in the world I wouldn't do for you."

"Ryan, you are very welcome for whatever it is you think I've done for you, but consider us paid in full. The things you are saying are crazy and just all too much for me to comprehend."

He laughed. "I'm sorry, I don't mean to make light of your concerns, it's just this is the first time since we met again that I seem to have you on the back foot and not in complete control."

"That's precisely my problem, Ryan. I don't do well when I'm not in control."

"But you are, don't you see that? Whatever future you and I do or do not have is entirely your call. I've told you how I feel and if you decide to act on that, all I'm saying is, I'll be around. If nothing else, I would hope that we could at least be friends. I'm going to be a little short of those when I move back here. I can't see your brother wanting to have a few beers and talk about old times, and he's the only other person I know here." He smiled.

She chuckled under her breath. "I think you have completely lost your mind, do you know that, Congressman?"

He wagged his finger at her. "Nah, ah, ah, not anymore. Somebody hasn't been paying attention. I'm no longer a congressman, or at least I won't be when I get back stateside and resign. You're going to have to find new ways to ridicule me from now on." He tapped her foot as if considering something. "Perhaps I'll become a farmer, what do you think?"

Monica giggled. "A farmer?"

"Yeah, why not?" He smiled. "I told you I like being outside and wanted to do something with my hands; I think being a farmer would be right up my alley. Farmer Whittaker," he said to himself to hear how it sounded. "I'm sure that has a certain ring to it. Do you think you would be able to call me Farmer and make it sound mocking?"

She pursed her lips as if thinking about it and trying to keep the amusement from her face. "Yes, I believe I could probably make that work."

"Well, there you go then, problem solved. Although, do you imagine it means that I'm going to have to start wearing tweed? I'm not sure if I can pull that off."

"Don't be such a pessimist. Of course, you can."

He raised his eyebrows. "You really think so?"

"Sure I do. Tweed with the leather elbow patches, I can see it now, Farmer Whittaker." She smiled.

He drew his eyebrows together. "You've started with the ridicule already, haven't you?"

She half shrugged. "No time like the present. I've never been one to let the grass grow under my feet."

"Something tells me you're not taking my new career seriously, Monica. If I don't see an immediate change of attitude from you," he wagged his finger at her again, "it's no free vegetables for you, and then you'll be sorry."

She giggled. "Well, seeing as we spend thousands each week on fresh produce, that would certainly serve me right."

"Indeed, it would. Just you wait until I've aced all my classes at Farmer College. Then you'll be laughing on the other side of your face, just you wait and see, young lady."

"Farmer College?" she chuckled. "I think they have one of those in town actually, right next to the Astronaut College."

His eyes widened with mock excitement. "Astronaut College, is that right? Now there's a thought that's going to fester. I wonder if I could go there at the same time on day release or night school or something, just to keep my options open, what do you think?"

"I think that makes perfect sense because you wouldn't want to put all your eggs in one basket."

"I've moved on from there, Monica, so stop talking about the chickens that are going to be on Whittaker Farm and let's talk about my spaceship, The Whittaker One!"

She laughed out loud. "And at what point are we going to talk about the straitjacket they are going to fit you for when everybody realises that you've lost your mind?"

"Will that have the leather elbow patches as well because I'm liking the sound of those?"

She continued to laugh. "For you, Farmer/Astronaut Whittaker, I will have one made specially."

"Will it be in tweed aluminium or whatever, just so that I can keep the same theme going? I don't want to get confused."

"I'll make sure of it," she confirmed.

"I'd appreciate that, Monica, thank you." He leant his head back, still smiling and closed his eyes. "Okay, so fair enough I'm not that brilliant with heights when I think about it, so maybe Astronaut College might be pushing it a little bit, but I don't care what you say, I think an ex-American congressman will make an excellent English farmer."

"Well, I certainly don't," came the stern voice of Annabel Whittaker from the doorway.

Monica stopped laughing immediately and rolled her eyes. "Oh, God, here she is," she drawled.

Annabel stepped further into the room, completely ignoring Monica and looked directly at her son. "I was told I might find you both here and it appears I got here just in time. What's all this talk of farming, Ryan, and what precisely do you mean by ex-congressman?"

Ryan took a deep breath. "The farmer part was a joke, mostly, but as for the rest, I'm done, Mother, I'm giving it all up and resigning from office as soon as possible."

"Resigning from office, over my dead body," Annabel fumed.

Monica nudged Ryan with her foot. "Please tell your mother that her terms are acceptable."

Ryan tried unsuccessfully to keep the smile from his face when he turned back to his mother. "I'm sorry, Mother, but my mind's made up. I'm finished with all of it, and I couldn't be happier about it."

"Then I suggest you just unmake your mind immediately, let's leave this place and put all of this insanity behind us. You'll feel better once you're not surrounded by all of these dreadful people."

Monica nudged him again with her foot. "On a scale of one to ten, how upset would you be with me if I were to throw my shoe at her right now? I'll even use my left hand and promise not to aim directly for her head just to give her a fighting chance."

Ryan patted her knee. "That's very sporting of you, Monica, but I'd really rather you didn't. Just leave it to me, I've got this."

"Are you quite sure, Ryan, because it's no trouble, I promise you," Monica teased.

"Quite sure, thank you."

"Yes, stay out of this, Monica, because it has nothing to do with you," Annabel snarled.

"Actually, Mother, that would be you. It's you that needs to stay out of this, and it's you that this has nothing to do with."

Annabel's eyes grew wide instantly until they looked like they were going to pop right out of her head. "What do you mean nothing to do with this? Anything that affects you directly affects me. I will not stand idly by and watch you throw your whole life away."

"Well, I guess that's up to you," he said calmly, as he stood and placed Monica's feet gently on the stone bench. "I've made my decision, and it's not up for debate, but what is still in question, however, is whether or not I allow you to remain part of my life, albeit in a very different capacity."

"Remain part of your life? Of course, I'm going to remain part of your life, Ryan, I will always be by your side, and what do you mean by *capacity*, you're not making any sense, dear."

"Then I suggest you listen to me and listen well. I'm done with congress, I'm done with politics, I'm done with America, and above all, I'm done with you, unless you start respecting my decisions and stop letting your own ambitions control my life."

Annabel's mouth fell open in shock. "Everything I've ever done has been with your best interests in mind, my son. Since you were a child, I've wanted nothing for myself, not once, I only wanted to see you succeed in being the best you could possibly be and achieve all of your dreams."

"But that's just it, Mother, they were never my dreams, they were yours!" he yelled.

Annabel took a step back at the impact of his words. "I...I don't understand where any of this is coming from, Ryan, I really don't." Her bottom lip started trembling and tears were building in the bottom of her eyes. "I know that I made a mistake with Nicholas today, a terrible mistake, but it's only a setback, Ryan, and I'm sure if we put our heads together there'll be some way out of this mess. Trust me, son, I'll find a way and I won't let you down again, I promise."

"You can keep your promises, and you can stop the tears, as neither of them means that much to me anymore," he said flatly.

Annabel took in a sharp breath. "You don't mean what you're saying, Ryan, you couldn't."

"I can and I do, Mother. I'm not playing by the rules anymore, well, not yours anyway. From now on I'm going to do whatever makes me happy, and if you can't accept that, then, well, I'm sorry but I just don't have any room in my life for you anymore."

"But...but...I love you." The tears that were building started to fall down her face. "I need you, Ryan, I need you with me." She grabbed hold of his arms and shook him to emphasise her point.

He took hold of her shoulders and held her away from him. "But I don't need you. I realise now that I never did. And if you love me, and ever want to have any kind of relationship with me again, the best thing you can do, the only thing you can do to help make that happen, is by going home and wait for me to contact you. I need some time apart from you and everything else connected to my old life if I'm going to make a fresh start."

"Don't do this, Ryan, please." Annabel sniffled.

"It's done, Mother, and it's not negotiable. Now do as I say and just go, will you please."

Monica started clapping rapidly from behind him. "Whoot, Whoot! You tell her, Ryan."

Annabel wiped the tears away with the back of her hand and glared at Monica. "You," she growled. "Don't think for one moment that I don't know that this is all your fault."

Monica smiled. "I really do hope so, Annabel. When Ryan said earlier that I was the instigator for his change of attitude it scared the life out of me, but when you say it, it sounds like a compliment, and I'll take it, thank you."

"I'll give you a compliment," Annabel screamed as she flew at Monica with her fingers extended like claws.

Ryan grabbed hold of his mother to stop her progress.

"Wow," Monica laughed as she sat up in readiness. "Let her go, Ryan. I'll give you good money if you just let her go."

Ryan was struggling to control an incensed Annabel. "I think we all just need to calm down here. Violence is not the answer."

Monica laughed. "Of course it is, or at the very least it will be fun. You're going to need to learn that, Ryan, if you want to be anything close to my perfect man," she teased.

Annabel stopped her struggling. "Perfect man?" She looked first at Monica then back at Ryan. "So this is all about her, isn't it?"

"It's about me, Mother. What I do from now on, everything I do will be just about me."

"About you indeed," she sneered. "She has got you so twisted around her little finger you can't even see straight. Just look at what you were doing when I came in, sitting there rubbing her feet like some sort of lapdog. What's next, Ryan? How low are you prepared to go for her?"

"As low as she wants me to, Mother. As low as she'll allow me to. I love her, and what makes her happy makes me happy."

"Oh, so you love her now, do you?" she scoffed as she shook her head in disbelief. "You're every bit as weak as your father was. What is it about the Montgomery men and the Katlyn women? Your father thought himself to be in love too. Do you know he actually thought he was going to leave me and run away with her mother? Leave *me*!" she screamed in full rant mode. "Leave me, with my background and connections, to play happy families with nothing more than a gangster's moll! Well," she shook her head in disgust, "I put a stop to it then, and I'll put a stop to it now, just you mark my words."

Ryan looked a bit shell-shocked. "What on earth are you talking about, Mother?"

"Yes," Monica slowly got to her feet. "What are you talking about, Annabel? How exactly did you put a stop to it before?"

Annabel smiled at her with pure venom. "How do you think?" She laughed like a mad woman. "Look at you, standing there, thinking you are so smart, so clever, well let me tell you something, you know nothing," she spat as she laughed again. "But the thing of it is, the best part is, that you actually do know, and you don't even know it?"

"She's not making any sense; I think we need to call a doctor," Ryan intervened.

"No, wait," Monica instructed, never taking her eyes off of his mother. "Go on, Annabel. Tell me what it is you think I already know."

"Well, you were there, dear, you really should be able to tell me. I know you were young but you were hardly a baby."

Monica took a deep calming breath realising that something monumental was about to happen. "I was there for what?"

Annabel shook her arm out of Ryan's grasp and took on a defying and challenging stance. "You were there when I killed your mother, and you were certainly there when I tried to kill you. If your brother and Ryan hadn't arrived precisely when they did, I would have succeeded with you too. Just another moment longer, and history wouldn't be repeating itself, and none of this nightmare would be happening right now."

Monica stumbled backwards to regain her seat as the full impact of Annabel's words sunk in. She doubled over, buried her head in her hands and cried out as she could practically feel something click in her brain and thirty years of repressing those memories suddenly disappeared.

Chapter Twelve

A five-year-old Rebecca Katlyn opened her eyes from a deep sleep and for a moment wondered what had awoken her. She still felt very tired, and she could tell through the gap in her curtains that it was still night-time outside so why wasn't she still asleep?

Looking around her bedroom with the aid of her night light, she could see her daddy asleep on the sofa on the other side of the room. It was a sight she was used to seeing and it always comforted her, even if he did always make that snoring sound, which seemed much louder tonight than it normally did. Perhaps that's what had woken her up?

She crawled out of bed and padded over to her father, crawling onto the sofa with him to cuddle into his chest. He mumbled something she couldn't understand and his arm came around her, holding her close.

He smelt funny, like the coloured bottles he kept in his billiard room on the shelf that he would always tell her she could try when she got older. Again she was used to the smell by now so took comfort in the familiarity.

She was just starting to drift off to sleep again in her daddy's arms when she heard running outside her bedroom door, and what she thought was her mummy's voice shouting at someone to stop what they were doing. Was Nicky in trouble again? According to her mummy, her big brother was always up to mischief. Rebecca decided she needed to go and investigate.

When she opened her bedroom door, there were a few lights on here and there, but the house now seemed to be totally silent. Holding onto the banister railings and taking each step one at a time like her mummy had taught her, she made her way down the large sweeping staircase.

When she got to the bottom, she still couldn't see or hear anybody, but she was cold because somebody had left the front door wide open and she was only dressed in her pyjamas.

She walked over to it to look outside.

Down the grass slope the other side of the trees she could see her mummy, standing in front of the swimming pool with her hands up in front of her, the way she did when her daddy was mad with her brother and she wanted him to calm down. Who was mad with her brother this time? Why was mummy by the pool when it was still dark outside, and she didn't even have her costume on? There was only one way to find out.

Walking across the lawn was fine although maybe a little wet, but when she got to the path that led through the trees she wished she had thought to put her slippers on. Eventually, though her progress was slow, she got close enough to hear voices.

"Anna, please." She heard her mother beg. "Just think about what you're doing."

Auntie Anna? Why was Auntie Anna mad with Nicky, unless of course she was mad with her mummy? Rebecca tried to increase her pace but stepped on a stone that dug into her foot. Unable to walk any further, she sat down on the damp dirt and started to pull all the debris out of her feet and wipe them as best she could before continuing her journey to whatever it was that her mummy and Auntie Anna were up to.

"Well, that's rich, coming from you, Lucille," Auntie Anna huffed. "When have you ever spared a thought for anything, or anyone, but yourself? Did you really think I didn't know about you and my husband? Did you think me that stupid that I was totally oblivious to what was going on right under my very nose? The two of you weren't nearly as subtle as you may have thought. It may have been enough to fool the idiot you married, but not me, *never* me."

"I'm sorry, okay," her mummy pleaded. "We never meant to hurt you, Anna, honestly, we didn't, and I know that we must have, terribly, but you can't do this. My children..."

"Will be better off without you," Auntie Anna interrupted. "No child deserves to be brought up by a whore!" she screamed.

"Derek!" her mummy called in desperation.

"Oh, save your breath," Auntie Anna instructed. "With what I put in your husband's last drink, he is going to be dead to the world until morning and won't remember a thing."

"You don't want to do this, Anna, not really."

Auntie Anna laughed. "Of course I do. I just shot my husband, your lover, in front of you, Lucille. Do you honestly think after that, there is any way I would let you live to tell the tale?"

"You won't get away with this, Anna. Surely you see that? The police…they'll know it was you, and they'll come after you. You'll go to prison, and you won't see your son grow up. Think about Ryan before you do anything else that is going to make this situation even worse."

"My son is precisely the reason why I'm doing this. Do you think I would allow him to grow up with the shame of having a father who would rather degrade his heritage to be with someone like you, rather than one of his own ilk? I could have had any man I chose when I was younger, but my father insisted that by marrying an English Lord, my future, and that of my children's, would be secure. We obviously didn't know that this particular Lord liked to roll around in the trash, and could potentially bring his whole family down with him. No, this will be much better for Ryan in the long run, than any long drawn out scandal."

"If you do this, he won't have a father or a mother. Scandal or no scandal, you'll be leaving him all alone in the world. Do you seriously want that for your only child?"

"That's where you're wrong. I won't be going anywhere, except away from this Godforsaken country and back home to America where I belong. Don't you recognise the gun I'm pointing at you right now, Lucille? You should you know, it belongs to your husband. It's surprising how chatty he gets sometimes, and how he likes to show me things that he thinks will shock me, especially after I've put his rancid dick in my mouth for a little while."

Lucille's sharp intake of breath had Anna chuckling.

"What?" She raised her eyebrows in amusement. "Did you honestly think that you and that worthless piece of shit of a husband of mine were the only two around here having any fun? Let me tell you, my dear; your husband can't get enough of me." She giggled. "He was more than happy to show me where it was he kept his gun, and was even sweet enough to show me how to use it, as you saw me demonstrate a short while ago. Now, given the fact that Derek Katlyn's cheating whore of a wife and her long-term lover will have been shot with his gun, a man of very questionable morals and a reputation for violence I might point out, do you really think anybody is going to look twice at little old me? I'll be able to play the part of the grieving widow to perfection; it is, after all, a role that I've longed for."

Rebecca, now feeling scared and bewildered herself, got back on her feet and continued forward. Breaking through the treeline, she saw her mummy's tear-stained face looking at her.

"Rebecca, run!" her mummy screamed at the top of her voice while lunging towards Auntie Anna.

Auntie Anna fired the gun once before running off into the trees, and her mummy dropped to the ground.

Rebecca didn't know what else to do so she ran to her mother's side. Kneeling on the ground beside her, she felt warm stuff starting to soak into her pyjama bottoms; she started shaking her mummy so she would open her eyes and tell her everything was going to be okay, but no matter what Rebecca seemed to do, her mummy wouldn't stir. The black gooey stuff was all down the front of her mummy's dress now, and Rebecca tried to wipe it away but it just covered her hands and stuck to her. She hugged her mummy close and cried into her shoulder, begging her to wake up but to no avail. Finally, she decided she needed to go and get her daddy to help her.

Back in her bedroom, she crawled all the way up her daddy's still sleeping body. She jumped up and down on him, tried to pry his eyes open with her tiny little fingers but the only thing she managed was to cover daddy in the same black gooey stuff as well.

Running back to the pool area to see if her mummy was somehow awake by now she stopped dead when she realised that her mummy was now in the water floating face down.

Rebecca stood by the poolside and started screaming for her brother. Surely Nicky would know what to do. She turned when she heard footsteps and almost cried out in relief.

"Auntie Anna, please help me. Mummy is asleep and won't wake up, and now she is in the water and she won't be able to swim."

"I know she is, dear, I kicked her in there myself. Just in case she survives the bullet, I thought I'd drown the bitch as well. I'm sorry, child, but you may have seen too much so now it's your turn."

Rebecca screamed as Auntie Anna pushed her into the pool alongside her mother. As she broke through the water she started gasping for air, Auntie Anna grabbed a handful of her hair and pushed her back under, holding her there and wouldn't let go.

She kicked her legs, twisted her little body and pulled on Auntie Anna's wrist but no matter how hard she tried she couldn't get away and she couldn't hold her breath any longer either.

With one final attempt at calling for her brother, which resulted in a string of bubbles leaving her mouth, Rebecca felt the grip on her head loosen and saw something break through the water.

The next thing she knew she was in her brother's arms, her legs wrapped around his waist, coughing and spluttering, and he had his arms around her and was cradling her head into the crook of his neck.

"Nicky, I'm scared," she blubbered. "I don't like this dream anymore; please make it stop."

"Shh, shh, shh, I've got you, Ecca," he comforted. "Don't look up, baby girl, just stay as you are and let your big brother take care of you now."

"I tried to get to her, Nicholas, to pull her out, but I just couldn't reach," Auntie Anna explained.

What? No, that wasn't right.

"It's okay, Aunt Anna, I have her now. I got up to get a drink and went to check on her like I always do and found my dad in there passed out covered in blood so I went back to my room and woke Ryan, then came looking for her." He planted a kiss on his sister's wet hair. "Thank God I found her. Ryan, help me get my mother out will you?"

"Perhaps it would be best to leave her where she is for now, Nicholas?" Auntie Anna ventured. "The police might prefer it, that nothing has been touched and everything is as we found it?"

"Police?" her brother enquired.

"Yes," she said cautiously. "I called them before I left the house. They should be here shortly."

"Did you call an ambulance as well?"

"Well, no. I wasn't completely sure what had happened before I got out here, I just knew something wasn't right and I thought it better to be safe than sorry."

"I don't care what the police want. I'm not leaving my mother like this. Ryan, get in here, now."

Ryan jumped into the pool and he and a one-handed Nick, as the other was still clinging to his baby sister whom he refused to let go of, lifted Lucille Katlyn's lifeless body from the water.

By the time the police had arrived, Nicky had stood in the warm shower with Rebecca still in arms, removed her wet, dirty clothing, washed her, dried her, then redressed her in fresh pyjamas before tucking her into his own bed.

He leant forward and kissed her forehead. "Sleep now, Ecca," he whispered. "Everything is okay now."

Rebecca took her big brother's face in her tiny hands. "But Nicky, what if I have the same horrible dream again? It was scary and it frightened me and I don't want to be scared anymore."

"Don't think about that dream anymore, Ecca, okay? Just forget all about it and know that I am here and that dreams can't hurt you, and even if they could, I will always protect you and keep you safe."

"You promise, Nicky, always?" she whined.

"Always, baby girl, I promise, now go back to sleep and trust me when I say that everything is going to be okay."

"I love you, Nicky," she breathed as she closed her eyes and settled into the pillows.

"I love you too, Ecca," he whispered.

Rebecca drifted back off to sleep, forgetting all about her previous dream, safe and protected in her big brother's arms.

Chapter Thirteen

Monica lifted her head from her hands and looked up at a demented looking Annabel and a stunned looking Ryan.

"It was you," Monica breathed, looking at Annabel. "All this time, I thought…I believed…but all along; it was you."

Annabel started chuckling. "Yes, that's right. It's all coming back to you now, isn't it? Better late than never, I suppose," she taunted.

"Can somebody please tell me what the hell is going on here?" Ryan demanded.

"It's quite simple, dear," Annabel responded. "Your father was going to leave me, so I shot him, along with her whore of a mother," she declared joyously as though proud of her actions.

Ryan slowly shook his head in disbelief. "Mother, you can't be serious? Why would you say such things?"

"Because they are true, and it's about time she realises just what I'm capable of, and that I am not somebody to be messed with, don't you think?" she gloated.

"You planned it all along so that my father would be blamed, didn't you?" Monica asked quietly.

Annabel beamed a smile. "Of course, I did, child. It wasn't personal because I quite liked your father, truth be told, but I needed somebody to take the fall and he was convenient, although I have to give credit where's credit due, you helped immensely with that."

"Me?"

"Absolutely. When I first realised that you had witnessed what I'd done, I understandably panicked. Firstly, because I didn't know if you were alone or not, and secondly, because I didn't know what you would say about what you had seen, or who would believe you. But low and behold the Gods were smiling on me that night, because not only did you not remember a thing, while trying to help your mother you covered your father in her blood, whereby, sealing the deal as it were." She clapped her hands together happily. "It was all just too perfect. I've always wanted to thank you for that, but until now, of course, I'd not been able to."

"I always thought they were just bad dreams. I didn't know it was all real, that it had actually happened," Monica said to herself.

"Well, now you do." Annabel smiled. "How does it feel to know you could have stopped your father going to prison, but didn't? My guess would be by the look on your face it's not that pleasant a realisation."

Monica started retching, so turned around, hanging her head out of one of the glassless windows and clinging to the stone ledge as if her life depended on it.

Annabel started to laugh. "So much for the big, bad, Katlyns. Just look at you now? The truth was just too much for your tiny little brain to hold onto, and now that you've remembered it all, it's too much for your constitution. How wonderfully...weak."

Monica eventually composed herself, and wiping her mouth with the back of her hand, turned to face Annabel again. "Why would you tell me this? Why on earth would you want me to remember? Surely you knew there would be repercussions if I ever found out the truth. Why would you put yourself in this situation?"

"And what repercussions would they be, my dear? What can you possibly do to me without your brother finding out? No matter how much he may seemingly protect you in front of others, we all know there is no love lost between the two of you anymore. If he were to find out your part in all of this, that you knew all along that his father was innocent and you didn't say anything and just stood by and let him get taken away from him, he'd kill you too, and we both know it."

"Yes, he would." Monica slowly got to her feet. "Ryan, if you want to say goodbye to your mother, I suggest you do it now."

Ryan looked confused. "You're just going to let her go? You're not going to call the police or anything?"

Monica's eyes went to Annabel and every muscle in her body started to twitch with the effort of holding her anger inside her. "She's not going anywhere," she replied with a shaking voice.

Ryan took a step backwards, closer to his mother, and raised his hands in front of him as a barrier. "Monica, you need to calm down before you do something you're going to regret."

A smile curved her lips but didn't reach her eyes. "I'm way beyond regrets, Ryan, and you need to get out of my way now."

He took another step back. "I can't do that, Monica. I know what she did was wrong, terribly wrong, but she is still my mother, and I can't just stand aside and let you hurt her."

She looked him straight in the eye. "Don't for one moment think you are even close to being in Vinnie's league, Ryan, because you're not and you won't be able to stop me. Now, your mother and I have some longstanding unfinished business, so, get - out - of - my - way."

"Monica, I..."

"Now, Ryan," she screamed.

Annabel started chuckling again. "Step aside, Son. What can she possibly do to me anyway? One mark on me and she'll have to explain to her brother why." She looked at Monica and grinned smugly. "You're not going to risk that, are you, my dear?"

Monica grinned back. "You know the difference between you and me, Annabel, apart from the glaringly obvious one in that you are one soulless, conniving, evil bitch? Firstly, for my part in all of this, my conscience tells me I deserve to die at my brother's hand, and I'm okay with that. Secondly, unlike you, I'm looking forward to seeing my parents again, so I am quite happy for us to go and see them together. I'm ready if you are, *my dear*?"

Annabel's face dropped. "Stop her, Ryan," she implored him and she put her hand on his back. "She's obviously gone completely mad, Son, so don't let her get near me."

He took another step back, taking his mother with him. "Monica, you need to calm down and listen to me. You've had a dreadful shock and you're not thinking clearly."

Monica took a step towards them. "Oh, I'm thinking clearly, Ryan. I know exactly what I need to do, so I will tell you one last time, for your own sake, get out of my way."

"I'm sorry, I can't do that, so if you want to get to her that badly, you are going to have to go through me," he said quietly.

She half shrugged. "If that's your decision, then so be it, but don't say I didn't warn you."

Monica charged at them both and Ryan pushed back so quickly Annabel lost her footing. She fell backwards and teetered on one of the stone windowsills, still holding onto Ryan, who continued to push back against her, putting himself between his mother and the imminent danger approaching them, unaware of the danger he himself was putting her in behind him. As Monica reached for them, he pushed back further, toppling Annabel completely who maintained her grip on him and they both plummeted out of the glassless window.

Monica instinctively grabbed for Ryan but was too late. Looking down at the ground four storeys below her, she could see them both laid there, unmoving, their arms and legs at unnatural angles. She knew without a doubt that if it had just been Annabel down there, she would leave her exactly where she was, but Ryan deserved better than that, and she had no choice but to help him if she possibly could, though she feared she would be too late. She turned away from the window and slowly walked out of the clock tower.

Chapter Fourteen

Monica sat in the hospital waiting room, her brother and Vincent either side of her. She hadn't said a word about what had happened, or more specifically, why it had happened, because she was biding her time waiting to hear that Ryan was going to be okay before she had what she assumed would be her last conversation with her brother.

Annabel had made it through the emergency surgery, but was critical yet stable, though still unconscious. Ryan, however, was still in surgery due to extensive internal injuries, and the doctors weren't hopeful for the outcome.

After what seemed like an eternity, a nurse approached them and advised them that Mrs Whittaker was awake now, and they could see her for a short while if they wanted to. Monica excused herself from the others and went into Annabel's room alone.

Annabel looked up at her from her bed in her drug induced haze. "Where's Ryan? Is my son okay? I asked the nurse, but she couldn't tell me anything so tell me now, is he all right?"

Monica leant back against the closed door and looked at the woman she considered to be responsible for everything wrong in her life. "He's still in surgery right now. The jury is out as to whether his is another death you can add to your tally, but it doesn't look good."

"Me?" Annabel looked indignant. "None of this would have happened if you hadn't behaved the way you did, like some sort of animal."

Monica smiled. "You genuinely believe that, don't you? You really think that none of this is your fault? How can you go through life, being as evil as you are, and yet feel so blameless?"

Annabel ignored her question. "And Nicholas? Is he here?"

Monica nodded. "He is. He's waiting outside."

"I take it you haven't spoken to him yet about what exactly went on in that clock tower?"

Monica shook her head. "Not yet, but I'm going to."

Annabel huffed. "If you were going to you would have done it already. What on earth would you be waiting for?"

Monica approached her bed and sat down on the chair beside it. "I'm waiting to see if Ryan makes it or not." She leant across and started straightening the covers on top of Annabel. "You see, I'm not quite ready to leave this earth just yet. I need to know that Ryan is going to be okay, and if not," she smiled again, "if he dies, then before I go, I'm going to kill you."

Annabel swallowed deeply. "You won't get away with it," she muttered. "We are in a public place now, and there are witnesses, somebody would see you."

Monica chuckled. "Do you really think I care? You have taken everything from me. My parents, my childhood, even the relationship I once had with my brother; it's all gone because of you. The mere fact that even to this day I can't stand to be touched and I know now it's because I remember so clearly you grabbing me and holding me under the water, all of it is your fault. Do you really think I'm going to let all of that slide without a reckoning?" She sat back in her chair. "Besides, as you quite rightly said earlier, as soon as I tell Nicky the truth about all of this, he's going to kill me anyway, so what do I care about getting caught or going to prison if I'm dead."

"What's to stop me from telling someone, so they call the police? Do you think I'm just going to lie here and wait for you to make up your mind whether I live or die?"

"I think that's exactly what you're going to do, because if you were to tell anybody, you would go to prison, and if there's one thing on this earth that you do care about, it's your own arse, so you'll wait, and take your chances."

A nurse entered the room to check on Annabel, and Monica got to her feet.

"You rest now, Annabel." She patted her shoulder. "I'll just be outside waiting for news about Ryan, and then I'll be back, I assure you." She smiled again and left the room.

Three hours later a doctor came to them to say that Ryan had pulled through the operation, and although he was weak, all signs indicated he should make a full recovery. He was still unconscious and they expected he would sleep through the night, and they should come back the following morning to see him.

The relief that Monica felt was immense although short-lived as now she had to deal with her brother.

She got to her feet. "Nicky, I want you to come to Annabel's room with me, please."

Nick drew his eyebrows together. "Why would I want to do that? You said we had to stay here to find out if they were going to be okay, and we have, so let's just go now."

"We can't," Monica informed him. "I need to tell you something, and it concerns her so I want her to witness the conversation."

Nick half smiled. "Is this the point that you tell me in front of her that you pushed that skank out the window because save your breath, Ecca, I already guessed that and I don't give a fuck. Why would I?"

"I didn't push her, Nicky. I probably would have given half a chance, but I didn't. She and I had a conversation for want of a better word, and she made me remember things I'd forgotten, and now you need to know them too."

"Like what?" He looked intrigued.

"Just come with me, would you please, and I'll explain everything as best as I can."

Both he and Vincent got to their feet, but Monica put a restraining hand on Vincent's arm.

"I need you to stay out here, Vinnie, and make sure we're not disturbed. Whatever you hear coming from that room, don't let anybody in there, okay?"

"What's going on, Moani?" Vincent looked concerned.

"It's just long overdue family stuff; that's all." She turned to walk away from him then stopped herself and turned back. "I love you, Vinnie, you know that, right?"

His concern grew. "Yeah, I love you too, but you're scaring the shit out of me right now. Tell me what's going on and maybe I can help?"

"Not this time, babe. This is all down to me and it's about time I faced it."

She hugged him closely, kissed him on the lips then took her brother's hand and led him to Annabel's hospital room.

Annabel awoke with a jump when Monica entered the room.

"What's happened?" she demanded. "Is Ryan okay? Is he...?"

"Ryan is going to be fine," Monica assured her. "But now it's time for you and me to have that reckoning we were talking about earlier."

Nick walked around Monica and stood the other side of Annabel's bed. "Well, you look like shit, Annabel. How are you feeling?"

Annabel looked nervously at Nick then at Monica, then back at Nick. "I...I..."

Nick started chuckling. "Don't sweat it, dear, it's probably the drugs they have you on that have you all turned around. You really should rest you know, but my baby sister seems determined that we all have a conversation right now. She assures me that it wasn't her that pushed you and Ryan out of the window tonight, which, I naturally assumed she had, so if it's not that, have you any idea what all of this is about, because quite frankly, she has me intrigued?"

Annabel looked back at Monica and swallowed deeply. "You don't have to do this, Monica," she said quietly. "It's all ancient history, and we should just let sleeping dogs lie."

"Oh, we're doing this, Annabel." She picked up the call button from the bed and put it on the bedside cabinet. "Let's just move that out of arm's reach to make sure we're not disturbed, shall we?"

"Nicholas, you can't believe a word she says," Annabel blurted out in a last ditch attempt to save her own skin. "She's demented, and she's a liar, and you should just take her away from here and never speak to her again."

Nick's jaw tightened. "I thought we already went over the rules about what's acceptable when talking about my sister, Annabel? I do so hate to repeat myself," he warned.

"But she's about to tell you a pack of lies, Nicholas," Annabel implored.

Nick looked at Monica. "I doubt that. She's never lied to me before, even at times when I would have probably preferred it if she had, so I don't think she'll start now. So, what's on your mind, Ecca? Whatever it is, Annabel obviously doesn't want me to know, so let's hear it."

Monica took a deep breath, licked her dry lips, and then recounted the entire story to him, all of her newly acquired memories from that night, including her involvement in implicating their father. Nick's face remained stone-like throughout.

When she had finished, she took a step towards him. "I don't want to insult you, Nicky, by telling you how very sorry I am. I know how inadequate that word is, but I mean it from the bottom of my heart. If there were any way that I could go back and change things, I would, but I know I can't. But I want you to know, that whatever you do to me now, whatever repercussions I have to face because of my actions, I don't blame you, and I don't begrudge you one second of your revenge."

He remained perfectly still for a few moments while reflecting on her words. Finally, he took a step towards her, closing the gap between them and put both of his hands around her throat.

She closed her eyes and swallowed deeply feeling her throat constrict against his thumbs, but instead of tightening his grip as she assumed he would, he rested his forehead against hers.

"What type of man have I become in your eyes that you would ever think you had anything to fear from me? Don't you know that I would die a thousand deaths; that I would burn in hell from now until the end of time, just to keep you safe?"

She opened her eyes to see tears building at the bottom of her brother's eyes. This mountain of a man that she believed to be incapable of feelings was humbling himself before her. Even after knowing the whole truth, he still loved her. "But...they took the father that you loved away from you, and I could have stopped it. How can you not hate me for that?"

"Nothing in this world is as important to me as you are, and nothing, and I mean nothing, could ever possibly make me hate you. Don't you understand that, Ecca?"

She put a hand on his face. "I do now. I don't think I've ever felt more loved in my entire life."

He took her in his arms and hugged her closely; then he pulled back to look at her. "But," he breathed looking at Annabel. "This cunt dies."

Monica smiled. "Yes, she does."

"But..." Annabel stammered, "you said if Ryan lived you wouldn't kill me?"

"No, what I said was that if Ryan died, I would kill you myself. He hasn't died, so I'm going to let my brother do it instead."

"He will know what you've done. After everything he witnessed this evening, he's not an idiot. He will know it was you and he'll never forgive you."

"That's okay, Annabel, because I would never insult him by asking him to. I think forgiveness can be overrated anyway, that's why you certainly aren't getting any," Monica assured her.

Annabel went to call out for help, but Nick put his hand over her mouth to silence her.

"Go and wait in the car for me, Ecca. I'll be down shortly."

"No," she said flatly.

"You don't need to be a part of this, baby sister, it's not who you are."

Monica looked at a terrified Annabel then back at her brother. "I am a part of it and it's exactly who I am and who I've always been, I'm just done denying it, that's all. I'm not going anywhere, Nicky. She took something from both of us, and I'm going to stand right here and watch you settle that score." She leant down to put her mouth beside Annabel's ear. "Say hello to my mum and dad for me when you see them, you evil bitch," she whispered.

When Monica and Nick left the hospital room, an anxious Vincent was waiting for them.

"What's all the commotion? Is everything okay?"

"Everything is fine now," Monica assured him. "Annabel didn't make it, though. Must have been post-op complications, don't you think, Nicky?"

Nick grinned. "Not so complicated really."

"Okay." Vincent looked at them both dubiously. "I'm guessing this is a story for when we are alone. Am I right?"

"You are," Monica confirmed. "Talking of which, can we please get out of here now? I'll come back in the morning to see Ryan."

Vincent put his arm around her shoulders. "Of course, we can. Come on, Moani Moani, I'll take you home."

"I don't want to go back to Eden tonight. I want to go back to my real home. Is it okay if I come back with you big brother?"

Nick smiled. "It's about fucking time."

Chapter Fifteen

Ryan was awake when Monica walked into his hospital room the following morning. He had one leg in plaster as well as one arm, and his other leg was in traction.

His face showed no emotion when he looked at her. "So, my mother didn't make it they tell me."

Monica sat down beside him. "No, she didn't."

"It's customary at times like these to offer someone your condolences. I'm glad you're not going to insult me by doing that."

Monica took a deep breath. "I can't tell you I'm sorry she's dead, Ryan, because we both know I'm not, but I am sorry for any pain that might cause you. Whatever she was or she wasn't she was still your mother and I know from personal experience how much that hurts."

"Were you with her when she died?"

"Yes," she said flatly.

He studied her face for a moment. "Do you think I'm an idiot, Monica?"

"No, Ryan, I don't. I never did."

"I fell out of a fucking window to stop you from getting to my mother, and now I'm supposed to believe that she just slipped away peacefully in her sleep while you just stood there and watched?"

"To be perfectly honest, Ryan, it doesn't matter what you believe, only what you can prove, which will be nothing."

"Is my mother's involvement in your mother's death and your father's incarceration common knowledge now?"

"No, nor is it going to be? Nicky knows, obviously, as does Vinnie, but we've talked about it and have decided that no good will come from dragging up the past. If you choose to tell anyone, that's your business."

"That's very generous of you both," he drawled sarcastically.

"To be honest, it is, but in the circumstances, I think it's the least we can do. There is no point in ruining the rest of your life over things that can't be changed. You can move on and let people think it was just a dreadful accident if that's what you choose to do."

"Move on? I didn't just scratch my new car, Monica, I lost my mother," he snapped.

"So did I," she snapped back.

He fumed in silence for a moment. "Why are you here? Surely any outstanding business we might have had has now been resolved."

"I wanted to see if you were okay."

"Am I supposed to believe you care?" he sneered.

"I care, Ryan, maybe more than you know. I would like to help, if you'll let me?"

"And how exactly can you do that?"

"I suppose that will depend on what you intend to do now. Have you changed your mind about leaving politics?"

"Do I want to reconsider being your brother's whipping boy, you mean? No thanks, I think I'll give that a miss."

"I've spoken with Nicky and whatever you choose to do moving forward, he won't interfere; he's given me his word."

"And I'm supposed to accept that, am I? The word of a Katlyn? I thought you said you didn't think I was an idiot?"

"What I think is that you're upset right now and not completely thinking clearly. Given time, you'll realise you do still have options."

"And what exactly would they be, Monica? Why don't you tell me all about my so-called options?"

"You could remain in office and go back to America, or, you could remain here…with me."

His eyebrows shot up. "Why would I want to stay here with you?"

"You said you loved me."

"I lied," he snapped.

She half smiled. "No, you didn't."

He let out a deep breath. "No, I didn't."

She leant forward and covered his hand with her own. "I can help you, Ryan. I know a little something about reinventing yourself after a tragedy, and I can guide you through it."

"You must be absolutely desperate for a new gardener, Monica. Are good staff really that hard to come by?"

She squeezed his hand. "I think we could probably do a little better than you being my gardener."

He looked at her before shaking his hand loose. "Thanks, but I think I'll pass if it's all the same to you. I'm done dancing to the Katlyn beat. From now on I'll make my own decisions."

Monica looked at him sadly then got to her feet. "Well, that's up to you, but the offer's there if you change your mind."

"I won't, and I don't want you to come back here either. Just stay away from me, Monica, please."

"If that's what you want?"

"It is. Looking at you reminds me of a life, that for a brief second, I thought I could have. I know now that I can't."

She leant down and kissed him on the mouth. "I'll always be there for you, Ryan, if you need me."

He looked her straight in the eye. "I'll never need you again."

She smiled sadly. "I hope with all my heart that that's true, I really do."

She gave his shoulder a gentle squeeze then left the room.

Epilogue

Elijah Stone sat at his desk in his corporate head office and looked up when his number two, Lee Temple, walked into his office.

"Lee, I want you to look into something for me. Have you ever heard of a place called Hotel Eden?"

"I have. Swanky place out in the sticks, why?"

"I thought I might have this year's charity bash there, but for some reason the owner isn't interested in taking my business. Her name is Monica Maxwell, and I need you to poke around a bit and find me some dirt on her so I can use it as leverage?"

Lee drew his eyebrows together. "Wouldn't it just be easier to find somewhere else?"

Elijah looked at him as though he had gone insane. "She said no to me, Lee. No…to me. You know how crazy that makes me."

"Have you tried charming her, Eli? Sometimes that works you know?"

"Actually, I did, but she won't even agree to meet with me. Just find me something I can use to make her a little bit more amenable, will you?"

Lee held his hands up in surrender. "Fine, whatever. Give me some time and let me see what I can find out."

Three weeks later

"I've got something on that Monica Maxwell you asked me to look into, Eli, but I don't think you're going to like it."

"Why?" Elijah asked without lifting his head or taking his eyes off of the financial report he was reading. "Is there nothing we can use?"

"I'm not sure yet, I still need to do some more digging, but there's some sort of connection between her and Nick Katlyn." Lee handed Elijah a photo of Monica and Nick at a restaurant taken the night before.

Elijah looked up and slowly smiled. "So that's why she doesn't want to do business with me because she's Nick Katlyn's current squeeze."

Lee shrugged. "Like I said, I don't know yet, but there's definitely a connection there, and by the look of that photo, a strong one. Don't you think it would be wiser to just back away from this one?"

"Are you shitting me, this is priceless. You know I never miss an opportunity to mess with that prick. How perfect would it be just to take her away from him? By the look of her in this photo, it wouldn't exactly be a hardship."

"No, she's easy on the eyes all right, but what if he genuinely cares about her? You sure you want to go to war over a piece of arse?"

Elijah half shrugged. "Yeah, why not. It's a slow week. I need more details, Lee. Find out all you can about her background and how long the two of them have been seeing each other. Fucking with Nick Katlyn just became number one on my to-do list."

"Fine, have it your way, but don't say I didn't warn you if this all goes tits up."

Five weeks later

Lee approached Elijah's desk holding up a file. "Chapter and verse on Monica Maxwell."

"It's about fucking time. What took you so long?"

"The lady in question covered her tracks incredibly well, and now I know why."

Elijah smiled. "I'm going to like this, aren't I?"

Lee raised his eyebrows. "You might, but I don't. She's not Nick's bird, Eli, she's his sister."

Elijah looked stunned. "You're telling me that the owner of Hotel Eden is the gangster princess?"

"In the flesh. If it were leverage you were looking for I'd say you have it in spades, the question is, do you think you should use it?"

"Why wouldn't I?"

"Don't you think fucking with the man's sister is a little bit too close to home?"

"Oh, fuck, Nick Katlyn," Elijah said dismissively. "This hasn't got anything to do with him anymore. No, this is about next year's charity ball. If she covered her tracks that well, she obviously doesn't want the truth to come out about who she actually is, which makes her perfect for a little blackmail. Use all your contacts and find out her itinerary for the next few months. I'm not going to approach her at her hotel, I want some neutral ground somewhere that her brother isn't likely to be." He smiled again looking down at the picture of Monica in the file. "Well, well, well. The gangster princess. You and I are about to become very well acquainted, Monica Maxwell."

The End

(Or is it?)

Family Buisness – DNA Trilogy Book 2

By Lynn Cook

Chapter One

Monica couldn't help the moan of ecstasy escaping her throat as the ice-cold vodka and tonic hit her taste buds.

Her close friend Vincent smiled at her from the adjacent sun lounger. "That good, huh?"

She returned his smile. "You have no idea. I can't believe I deprived myself of alcohol for so long because now we are becoming quite good friends."

"So, no more bad dreams when you drink?"

Monica took another mouthful before placing the condensation covered glass on her side table. "The funny thing about bad dreams, when you realise they are in fact memories there's nothing to fear in them as you've already lived through them. That," she smiled, "and it was a little liberating to realise that after thirty years of thinking that my father killed my mother he was...well, I wouldn't go so far as to call him innocent, but he wasn't the man I had thought he was either."

Vincent drew his eyebrows together. "Not to rain on your parade, Moani Moani, but he was still a ruthless bastard."

She gave him a wink. "Aren't we all, from time to time?"

"You do amaze me with how quickly you have come to terms with everything that's happened."

Monica shrugged. "Why wouldn't I? The way I see it, it's a gift. I now know that while my parents obviously had a hugely fucked up marriage, my father loved both my mother and me despite his faults, and the man I believed my brother to be had me convinced that he was going to kill me for my involvement in his father's demise, and instead, he embraced me with open arms and I've never loved him more."

"Again, for fear of being the naysayer, this enlightenment you now cherish did come at the price of a woman's life."

"That depends on your perspective, Vinnie. The way I choose to see it is that a murdering bitch got what she deserved."

He half smiled. "I'm glad you see it like that, I really am, I just worry that there's more to it that you're not admitting to, even to yourself."

"What do you mean by more?"

"I don't know, Moani, more emotion maybe, some sadness, maybe some regret? I know deep down you think you killed her."

"That's because deep down I did. I could have kept my mouth shut but I chose not to, knowing she would die, and yet I'm managing quite nicely to live with that fact. If it's any consolation, I do feel bad for Ryan. If anyone ended up with the shit part of the deal, it was him. He came to me for help and didn't deserve to have his life upended like that."

"Have you heard anything from him?"

She shook her head. "Not since I left him in his hospital room a year ago. He asked me to stay away from him so I did. From what I can make of it, he has dropped off the face of the earth. His political career is over; his fiancé left him, and even if she was a worthless piece of shit, he lost his mother, which was the only real family he had left."

"Have you thought about reaching out to him?"

She slowly nodded her head. "I thought about it many times, but in the end, I didn't really see the point. I offered him my help and he turned me down flat, which was probably for the best. It's not like I would have been able to fix him, if anything, I could have ended up making matters worse."

Vincent looked thoughtful. "Do you know something, there was a time back then with how strenuously you stood his corner, and how much you were prepared to put yourself out for him, that I genuinely thought you were starting to care about the man."

"I did care about him, and I still do to a certain extent, but not enough to do either of us any good. It's not something I'm capable of. I'm still 'she with the frozen heart' and that's not likely to change anytime soon."

"I think that's a little harsh, Moani."

She smiled. "Of course you do, darling, that's because you are one of the very few people on this earth that I do love, but let's be honest, Vinnie, I may be ecstatic over having my family back together, be they alive or dead, but it doesn't change the fact that I'm not just damaged, darling, I'm broken, and we both know it."

He reached for his drink. "Well, I'll reserve judgement on that. I don't see someone as wonderful as you, growing old alone. You have too much love to give the right person and I don't agree that you can't be fixed."

"That's because you love me too, so won't accept what you know for a fact to be true."

He sat up throwing his legs over the side of the sun lounger to face her. "I think a big first step in fixing you would be for you to stop all this procrastinating. How many times are you going to drag me to this island, to this hotel, before you buy it? You love this place so buy it already."

Monica's face took on a contented look as she gazed around the pool area of the five-star St Lucian hotel that she had come to adore. "I must admit, the more I come here with you, the more I want it."

"So what's the problem? If you're short on funds, you know your brother will give you anything you need."

"No, it's not the money; I've more than got that covered."

"So what is it then? Are you worried about leaving Eden?"

A guilty look passed over her face. "Not worried exactly, because I know Willi would do a phenomenal job in running it for me. It's just for the longest time Eden has been my home, and my sanctuary, and epiphanies notwithstanding, I'm not sure if I'm comfortable walking away from it just yet."

"You won't be selling it, Moani Moani. You would still be able to go back there any time you wanted to."

"I know, but it wouldn't be the same. The changes I'd want to make here would take up a lot of my time, so I guess I'm feeling a little bit like I'd be leaving home."

Vincent chuckled. "You're scared, aren't you? Well, I never thought I would see the day."

"Oh, shut up, gay boy, what do you know?" She playfully punched his arm.

"Talking of which, did you see that new waiter last night? He was very easy on the eyes."

Her face went serious. "Vinnie, if I am going to buy this place, you really do need to stop shagging all the staff."

"I only shag the gay ones," he defended.

"Well, stop it. It's embarrassing, or it will be if they ever do work for me and they've all had carnal knowledge of my best friend."

"So, stop dicking around and buy the place, and I'll stop shagging the staff."

Monica contemplated his words. "How about we go into town this evening, then that way we can both get laid without compromising my professional ethics?"

"Deal." He high fived her. "It will do you good to get some action. Work out a few of those kinks."

"I get plenty of action and am kink free, thank you very much."

He grinned. "Battery operated implements don't count."

She looked shocked. "Since when? An orgasm's an orgasm whether you're with something with a pulse or not. Besides, occasionally I'm with something with the power of speech; I'm just never really very interested in what they have to say. Plus, you know my rule about trying never to have sex with the same man twice. I just like to hit and run, but with the hours I work it makes my options very limited."

He raised an eyebrow at her. "Some mistakes are worth repeating in my opinion."

"That hasn't been my experience for the most part, but I will take it under advisement." She laid her head back and pulled her sunglasses over her eyes.

They were both silent for a while and Monica felt herself drifting away with the sun beating down on her and an overall feeling of relaxation all around.

"I don't fucking believe it," Vincent said under his breath interrupting her mind-wanderings.

"Can't believe what?" she mumbled, not even bothering to open her eyes.

"Do you remember you asked me some time ago about a guy called Elijah Stone?"

"The guy that wanted to book Eden for the weekend for some charity thing? I remember. Wasn't there some bad blood between him and Nicky or something?"

"There was, and there still is, and he's sitting right over there at the bar."

"Really, where?" She looked up, deciding this finally warranted her attention.

"White shorts, loose sleeveless t-shirt, dark hair, goatee beard."

Monica lifted her sunglasses and zoned in on her target. "Wow - talking of getting laid, he's yummy. He should have included a picture when he was trying to browbeat me into accepting his booking. It wouldn't have made any difference from a business perspective, but it might have got him the dinner date he wanted. Is he single by any chance, or is there a wife kicking around here somewhere?"

Vincent raised his eyebrows at her. "Yes, he is single as far as I know, and no you can't because Nick would have a shit fit. He won't even like you being this close to him. I think we should leave, right now."

"Oh, stop being such an old woman. Besides," she sat up. "Nicky isn't here and what he doesn't know won't hurt him."

Vincent looked dubious. "You're playing with fire, Moani. When I say there's bad blood, I mean there's really bad blood. People get hurt when your brother and Elijah go head to head. I know you don't want to know the details and have never had any part of that side of Nick's life, but walk away from this, Moani, I'm begging you."

Monica smiled. "See, you say things like that and you make him sound almost irresistible."

Vincent went to say something but she stopped him.

"Don't get carried away, I'm only joking, kind of, but answer me one question? Does he know who you are?"

"I have no way of knowing that, Moani, but if I were a betting man, I would have to say yes, for the same reason that I can tell you the guy sitting down at the table right near him is Lee Temple, his number two, and the four on the table next to him are part of Stone's permanent goon squad. For fuck's sake, I knew we should have brought a few guys with us."

Monica half laughed. "Will you listen to yourself for a second? There's not always a conspiracy behind every door. Even if he does know who you are, what's the big deal? He's hardly going to order his boys to open fire right here, poolside. Don't you people wait for dark alleys for that sort of thing?"

"Moani, this is serious."

"No, I'm sure it's not." She got to her feet and wrapped her sarong around her bikini bottoms. "What this is, is a professional hotelier, which has just seen a potential client that she was unable to accommodate, so she would like to go and apologise in person. The rest is all your's and Nicky's bullshit and none of my business." She started slipping her feet into her flip-flops.

"I don't like this, Moani," Vincent persisted.

"What's not to like? I'm going to go over there, flutter my eyelashes and do the whole 'I'm sorry about your booking, Mr Stone' thing, while getting us both another drink. If he's as arrogant as most self-made men I know, he'll probably flip me the finger and it will be the shortest conversation in history."

Vincent looked unconvinced. "You really don't know how fucking gorgeous you are, do you? I'm gay, but if you weren't my best friend even I'd be tempted to do you."

"Ah, that's so sweet. If you weren't my best friend I'd be tempted to let you." She bent and kissed him full on the lips, which was always their way. "You sit tight, my darling, and I'll be back in a jiff."

As she approached the bar, Elijah Stone was engrossed in the newspaper in front of him. The bar staff that were all acquainted with Monica because of her regular visits greeted her warmly.

Pablo, the head barman, always served her personally whenever possible, having heard the longstanding rumours that she may very soon be his new boss.

"Miss Monica, you know you only have to wave and we would have waited on you by the pool." He spoke to her in his native French, which was how they always addressed each other.

She answered him in English, knowing he was also fluent. "That's quite alright, Pablo. I actually have an ulterior motive in coming over here. Mr Stone," she turned towards Elijah gaining his attention and extended her hand, "I'm Monica Maxwell, the owner of Hotel Eden. You had a business request for me about a year ago, one I'm afraid to say I was unable to fulfil. This is the first time our paths have crossed so I wanted to apologise in person, and if you'll allow me, buy you a drink in the spirit of no hard feelings."

Elijah's eyes went from hers to her extended hand which he took and held, and then back to her eyes. "You think this is the first time our paths have crossed, Miss Maxwell?"

Monica was a little too preoccupied with the deep brown eyes, and full pink lips, not to mention the East End edge to his voice that her roots wouldn't let her ignore, that she nearly missed the question. Yummy indeed, she thought to herself again. "Are you saying that we've met before, Mr Stone, because I think I would have remembered?"

"Met, no, that's not what I said, but I guess it's irrelevant for now. Please, take a seat, Miss Maxwell, I would be happy for you to buy me a drink, providing of course that you let me return the favour and buy you the next one?"

Monica smiled flirtingly, as she took the stool next to him. "Well, let's see how the first one goes; I am on holiday after all."

"Meaning?"

Monica half shrugged. "I don't mind doing my PR bit for the sake of my business, but if you start to bore me, then we're done."

He laughed. "You are very forthright, Miss Maxwell, so how about we lose the title bullshit, and I call you Monica and you call me Elijah?"

"Absolutely," she agreed. "Pablo, another beer for my new, hopefully, non-boring friend, Elijah, here, and another vodka and tonic for myself. Could you also have another beer taken over to Vinnie by the pool?"

While Pablo set about his task, Elijah looked over in the direction of Vincent, then back at Monica. "Where I come from, Monica, a man doesn't take too kindly to his woman sitting with another man?"

"How do they feel about their best friends sitting with another man where you come from, Elijah?"

"That would depend on the man."

"Then providing you're not some secret serial killer, I'd say we're rolling in puppies." She accepted her new drink with a smile of thanks to Pablo. "But we digress. Tell me, did your charity function go well at your alternative location?"

"Well enough. It lacked a certain ambience that I'm sure Eden would have supplied."

She grinned. "I'm sure it would have. What charity was it for again, I can't recall?"

"Underprivileged children."

Her grin widened. "That was it. Know a lot about going without, do you, Elijah?"

"I know enough."

"Really? Nice watch, by the way. Rolex?"

He smiled. "I didn't say I knew about going without recently. Besides, regardless of my situation, I'm doing a good thing. What exactly was your objection?"

"Notoriety. Your functions have something of a reputation, not to mention the publicity that inevitably follows. Guests of Hotel Eden expect a little more discretion."

"You shouldn't knock it until you've tried it. A good time is usually had by all, and we do raise a lot of money for charity."

"I don't doubt it. Include me on the invitation list next time and I'd be delighted to attend. I can be quite generous when properly entertained."

Elijah leant a little closer towards her. "I'm going to hold you to that, Monica Maxwell."

Monica leant in closer as well. "I look forward to it, Elijah Stone."

He raised an eyebrow. "Are you flirting with me, sweetheart?"

"I'm thinking about it because you are very pretty."

"You be sure to let me know when you decide."

Monica took a mouthful of her drink. "You'll know, don't worry."

He edged closer still. "Am I pretty enough to get you to reconsider and let me hold next year's charity ball at Eden?"

Monica smiled. "You don't hear the word 'no' very often, do you, Elijah?"

"Hear it, yes, accept it, never."

She put a hand on his knee. "Then today is not going to be a good day for you, pretty boy, because you are going to have to let this one go."

He covered her hand with his own. "I've got a feeling today is going to be an exceptional day, although your friend keeps looking over here, and he's not happy. My guess is the friendship only thing you feel is not reciprocated."

"Then, you would be mistaken."

"How can you be so sure?"

She smiled. "Because he may very well want to jump one of us, but it wouldn't be me. You would be much more his type."

Elijah took a few seconds to register what she had said. "Oh, right. So, genuinely just friends then?"

"Best friends," she corrected him.

"In which case perhaps we can discuss the other no I got from you. I seem to remember a dinner invitation that was flatly refused."

"I remember a dinner invitation with ulterior motives to get me to change my mind about your booking."

"Then let me rectify that now by repeating my invitation without the ulterior motive. Have dinner with me this evening?"

"Are you flirting with me now?"

"Absolutely, it's because you're very pretty too."

She smiled. "I'm not going to change my mind you know."

"About Eden, or about dinner?"

She drained her glass and Elijah went to raise his hand to attract the barman's attentions but she grabbed his wrist to stop him.

"Wait. I have a proposition for you."

"I'm listening."

"Play me at pool. If you win, I'll have dinner with you."

"And if you win?"

"Then I won't, and I'll tell everyone that I bitch-slapped you all around the pool table and made you cry."

He raised his eyebrows. "So, no pressure then. Where's the table?"

"They don't have one here at the hotel. You'll have to take a walk with me down the beach. There's a bar about five hundred yards down."

"Something tells me your friend is going to object strongly to you walking off with someone you've just met?"

"I'm sure he'll object quite strenuously. What about yours?"

"Mine?"

"The guy sat at the table behind you that is trying desperately to look anywhere but at us but is aware of your every move. Either he works for you, or you've got yourself a stalker."

He grinned. "I'm impressed."

She winked at him. "You ain't seen nothing yet. Wait till I kick your arse at pool. That will be really impressive."

Elijah got off his stool. "So, lead the way and let the arse-kicking commence."

"I'll just get my bag."

As Monica approached Vincent on the sun lounger, he lifted his sunglasses to look at her.

"That didn't seem like the shortest conversation in history to me."

"It isn't over yet." She bent down and picked up her bag. "We're going down to the beach bar to play pool."

"Are you shitting me? The man is dangerous, Moani, don't you get that?"

"I'm no threat to him, Vinnie, so what possible reason do I have to be afraid of him?"

He tried to respond but she spoke over him.

"We both know I'm going to do this, Vinnie, so stop being a pain in the arse about it. Also, you might have to entertain yourself tonight, as with any luck, I'll have dinner plans."

"Oh, this just keeps getting better and fucking better."

She bent down and kissed him on the mouth. "Laters, loser."

"Don't come crying to me when you're lying dead in a ditch somewhere."

"I'd haunt your arse from here to eternity." She winked and walked away.

Elijah was waiting for her at the end of the pool. "Problems?"

"Nothing I can't handle. So long as I'm not out past curfew he's promised not to hold back any of my pocket money."

"That was decent of him. What's with you two kissing on the lips? Are you sure he's gay?"

"Did you see any tongues?"

"No," he responded.

She smiled. "Then, yes, he's gay."

He smiled. "You're starting to fascinate me a little bit, Monica Maxwell."

"If it's only a little bit, Elijah Stone, I'm going to have to up my game."

As they walked into the crowded bar, the owner greeted Monica warmly.

"Miss Monica, you come to see us again, a pleasure as always. The pool table is being used right now, but I will go tell them to finish their game and it will be all yours. In the meantime, your usual?"

"Yes please, Fitch, and a beer for my friend, if you would be so kind."

"Take a seat, both of you and I will be back momentarily."

Once they were seated, Elijah gave her a questioning look. "I take it you come here often?"

Monica looked around the wood and bamboo shack with fixtures and fittings that had all seen better days. "I like it here. Don't get me wrong; I enjoy the luxury of the Don

Carlos, but I also like to get down and dirty in authenticity as well. I'm surrounded by millionaires most days, so coming to places like this, mixing with real people; it's kind of a treat."

"Because we all know that millionaires are complete wankers, right?"

"Complete wankers, yes, though I don't mind the pretty ones quite so much." She nudged him with her shoulder.

"But you don't feel bad when the so-called real people get kicked off the pool table because you've walked through the door?"

"God, no. It's push or be pushed in this life and I try to avoid the latter at all costs."

She accepted her drink with thanks to Fitch and assurances from him that the pool table would be free to use shortly.

"To be honest," she continued, "I don't tend to waste my time feeling bad about any of my actions. They're mine so I own them."

"I can understand that. What I am confused about, is why everyone you meet seems to treat you like royalty? Do you hold incriminating pictures on all of them, or what?"

"Nothing nearly so interesting. I get the red carpet treatment for the oldest reason in the book - money."

"I've got money but they're not all kissing my arse like they're kissing yours?"

"No, but the boys at the Don Carlos have heard the rumours that I'm thinking about buying the place, so they see me as their next boss."

"And here?"

"As and when I do buy the hotel, Fitch wants me to buy this place as an extension for the all-inclusive hotel guests and keep him on as manager."

"And will you?"

She shrugged. "Probably. As I said, I like it here."

"So Eden is going international. Will that be another place I'm barred from when you buy it?"

"You're not barred from Eden, just your hedonistic parties are."

"Hedonistic? Things might get a little wild to help loosen the purse strings a bit, but they're not that bad."

"When your hospitality department first enquired about booking Eden and I was looking into your previous events, there was a picture of you lying practically naked on the floor, surrounded by exotic dancers who were pouring champagne all over you, and one of them was sitting on your face."

He beamed a smile. "Yeah, that was a good one."

"I'm sorry I missed it, but if it's all the same to you, I'd rather you take your business down the street. God, you certainly do have a problem with the word no, don't you? Let it go already."

He smiled as he took a mouthful of his beer. "So, tell me about yourself?"

Monica laughed. "You make it sound like an interview. I'm telling you now, whatever position you had in mind, you couldn't afford me."

"I'm beginning to think that no matter the price, you'd be worth it."

"Oh, I know I'm worth it." She grinned. "The pool table is free. You go and rack them up and I'll get us another beer."

While Elijah set about his task, Monica waited at the bar. Beside her were two young men, both wearing American college t-shirts, cut-off jeans and scowls on their faces directed at her.

"Problem boys?" she enquired innocently.

"Yeah, princess, I've got a problem." The taller one of the two answered. "Why is it that me and my buddy here get kicked off the goddamn pool table just so you and Prince Charles over there can play?"

Monica smiled sweetly. "There could be many answers to your question I suppose, but why don't we just say that it's because God loves me more than you and leave it at that."

"It sucks, lady." The shorter one ventured.

"I'm sure it does, so how about I buy you guys a couple of beers to make up for it, and my friend and me will be out of your hair in about half an hour? Sound good?"

Neither of them spoke.

"Is everything okay, Miss Monica?" Fitch enquired.

"Everything is fine, Fitch. Can I have two more beers for me and another two for my disgruntled friends over here?"

"You want I should ask them to leave?"

"I'm sure that won't be necessary, will it boys?"

"No, man." The taller one held his hands up to Fitch. "We're cool. Just getting acquainted with the lady is all."

Fitch glared at them like he didn't believe a word of it but handed over the beers Monica had bought them anyway.

"There now, isn't it so much better when we all just get along?" She picked up her beers and turned to walk away.

"Bitch."

She heard this mumbled behind her. She hesitated momentarily and contemplated a response but decided against it.

Elijah was waiting by the pool table with pool cue in hand. "What was that about?"

"It appears I'm not the only one who doesn't like being pushed around. The previous players are a little bit pissed off at me for being booted off the table."

He drew his eyebrows together. "Why, what did they say?"

"Nothing of any consequence, I took care of it."

He looked over at the two young men at the bar who were still glaring at Monica.

"Yo, Rambo," she called while clicking her fingers to regain Elijah's attention. "There's only one way you need to prove your manhood to me and it's right in front of you, so quit stalling and break already. Let's say best out of three."

He gave one final look in the direction of the bar then bent and took his shot.

As Elijah potted the black on their second game, he looked up at Monica with a smirk.

"Don't get cocky, pretty boy, that's only one game each. There's still everything to play for. I just hope you don't lose your nerve under the pressure."

"That's never been a problem for me."

"But have you ever played for such high stakes before. Your reputation could be in tatters, a laughing stock amongst your peers, never able to show your face in public again."

"The fact that you are trying to psyche me out right now tells me you're not as confident as you're pretending to be."

"I'm just messing with you." She winked.

"I'm aware of that. You set them up while I go get us another drink."

As she was bending over retrieving the potted balls, she heard someone approach.

"I've gotta say, you may be all sorts of a stuck up bitch, but you sure do have a mighty fine butt."

Monica turned to see the taller guy from the bar standing in front of her.

He ran his eyes up and down her body. "Nice rack too."

"Don't do this," she said flatly.

"Don't do what?" He took an unsteady step towards her.

"I'm asking you nicely to walk away. I won't ask you nicely again."

"What's the problem? When I see a fine piece of ass, I feel it's my duty to point that out."

"Oi, arsehole. The lady told you to piss off. I suggest you take her advice."

Monica looked over her shoulder at Elijah. "I've got this, pretty boy." She turned back to the tall guy. "You are about thirty seconds away from having a really bad day."

"Oh, come on now. Wouldn't it be better if we all just got along?" he said sarcastically mimicking her while raising his hands.

She took a step back. "Don't touch me, big guy. I don't like it when people touch me."

"What - like this?" He poked her shoulder with his index finger.

Monica's face turned to granite. "Yeah, exactly like that."

Before the tall guy could see it coming, Monica drew back her right arm and punched him in the face and his nose started gushing with blood. As he staggered back, hands going to his face, she leant her hands back against the pool table, drawing both her feet up, which she planted with all her might directly into his stomach. He flew backwards, landing in the middle of a table that shattered all around him.

"And for the record, arsehole, my friend is much better looking than Prince Charles, no disrespect to my future king intended."

As Monica turned, she saw the shorter guy running towards Elijah with a beer bottle in his hand. Acting on instinct, she picked up a ball from the table and launched it directly at his head. He fell in a heap on the floor.

Elijah just stood there with a stunned look on his face.

Fitch came running over. "I knew these two were trouble as soon as I lay eyes on them."

"I'll leave you to clean this up, Fitch. Put the damages on my tab."

"Don't you worry, Miss Monica, I will take out the trash."

She kissed him on both cheeks and walked over to Elijah. "I think that's enough real people time for one day, pretty boy, let's go."

She led him out by the arm but only managed a few steps down the beach before he stopped, forcing her to stop and face him.

"What the fuck was that?" He still seemed a little shell-shocked.

Monica half shrugged. "Would fun be the wrong answer?"

"Fun?" He sounded incredulous.

"He touched me. I told him not to but he did it anyway. Nobody touches me without my permission," she defended.

"You are a fucking lunatic, Monica Maxwell, do you know that?"

Monica half smiled. "Does that not work for you, Elijah Stone? I'd heard you had a pair."

"You heard right. Please tell me that I have permission to touch you because I really need to kiss that beautiful, smart mouth of yours right now."

She tilted her head to the side. "I'm not that big on kissing, Elijah. It always seems like a waste of time to me."

"Put it this way, sweetheart. Something of mine has got to be inside something of yours, and since the only other option is fucking you right here and now up against that shack we just left, I'm guessing my tongue and your mouth is going to have to do."

She raised an eyebrow. "Do you always make such bad choices when given only two options?"

He smiled as he took a step closer to her. "Permission or not, I don't care if you do kick the shit out of me, I've got to kiss you, right now."

He grabbed her face with both hands and slammed his mouth against hers. Monica was a little taken aback but the feel of his lips on hers had her reaching for his hair and opening her mouth to enter into a fencing frenzy with his tongue.

He ended the kiss with a peck on her lips then pulled back slightly to look at her. "You might very well be my perfect woman."

"There's not too much perfect about me, Elijah, and considering you just called me a fucking lunatic; it says a lot about your character that you would think otherwise."

He ran his hand down her throat and around to grasp the back of her neck. "I came to terms with my character and the kind of man I am a long time ago, sweetheart."

"And what kind is that?"

He smiled slightly. "I think you already know."

She ran her fingers through his hair. "I think I do too."

"So what happens now with your proposition? What does your rule book say happens when it's a draw because one of the contenders decided to beat the crap out of someone and smash the place up?"

"Well, seeing as this seems to be the day that I'm breaking my own rules," she gently kissed his lips. "It says I'll meet you in the bar at eight."

Printed in Great Britain
by Amazon